THINGS I WANT BACK FROM YOU

Things I Want Back from You

stories

Elizabeth Stix

Black Lawrence Press

Copyright © Elizabeth Stix 2023
Executive Editor: Diane Goettel
Book Cover and Interior Design: Zoe Norvell

ISBN: 978-1-62557-074-1

Published 2024 by Black Lawrence Press.
Printed in the United States.

Some of these stories appeared in a slightly different form in the following publications:

Los Angeles Times Sunday magazine ("Things I Want Back from You"), *McSweeney's Quarterly Concern* ("The Acorn"), the *San Francisco Bay Guardian* ("Alice"), *Alaska Quarterly Review* ("Your Feedback Is Important"), *Tin House* ("The Bear"), *The Tusk* ("Crossing Log"), *Eleven Eleven* ("Exit Strategies"), *The Southampton Review* and the anthology *Best Microfictions 2019* (an excerpt from "Five Kinds of Disaster," as "Tsunami"), *The Fabulist* ("Guiseppe and Emiline"), She Reads ("While I Am Away"), *The Racket Journal* ("Toreador"), *The San Franciscan* ("Sleeping Giants in the Daylight"), and *Boulevard* ("Resurrection Man").

Drawings by Jeffrey Freymann.

For my mother
Harriet Jean Stix

and my father
Philip Mordecai Bernstein

Contents

Part One

Part Two

Part Three

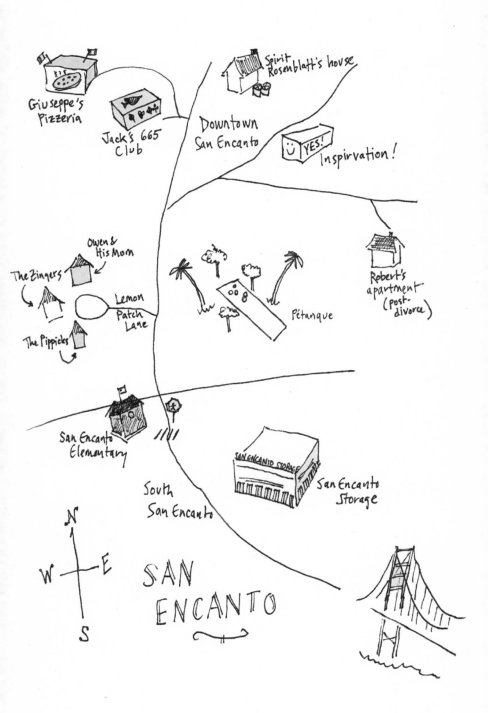

Part One

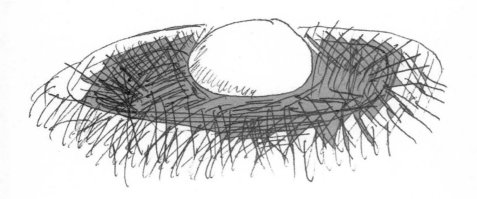

THINGS I WANT BACK FROM YOU

Fergus —

The following items belong to me:

1.   My cell phone case. It's blue with white sequins and I left it on the dresser by your closet. My carpal tunnel has completely flared up because it pinches my ulnar nerve to hold the phone when I walk and talk. I need the phone case back right now.

2.   My instant dog bath washcloths. Niffy is stinky and I think it is bothering her and it is definitely bothering me and I won't have time to give her a bath until Saturday. You know she produces more oil when she's itchy, and it's flea season. The cloths are in the drawer above the dishwasher.

3.   The photos from the Gualala trip. Please burn me a CD. I don't want to have to download them so please don't send them via email. I want them all, not just the ones I took. I was there and I want to have them all.

4.   My black backpack. It's on the floor of your office. Please just put it aside and don't dig through it. Please have some

respect for my privacy. It's just my papers from work but I have signed client confidentiality agreements and I would appreciate it if you would honor that, even though you didn't honor any of our other agreements. Perhaps a legally binding agreement such as the ones I signed with my clients will mean more to you than the promises you made to me.

5.   In the bathroom: on the shelf above the sink: my eye-drops. I have to put them in every night or I wake up with scratchy eyes, and I have not been sleeping well so my eyes are even drier. I can buy more but I don't see why I should have to when the bottle is only half used. Also on the shelf: my saline solution. (Please stop using it if you have been. Use your own.) My glasses case. And on the windowsill, I left a Chapstick.

6.   If you're not going to use the exercise ball, I would like to have it. You can keep it if you are using it.

7.   My black felt pen. It's on your desk next to the computer, or it least it was when I left. It's my favorite pen and I can't remember the brand so even if you think this is petty I do want it back. If you are using it, I would appreciate it if you would stop, or at least make sure that the cap is on securely when it is not in use.

8.   This is something you will probably not agree with. But I want some money for therapy. I have been talking about you for six sessions straight now, and I don't think it's fair that I should have to pay for it. If you had not slept with Daylene, I would not be wracking my brain trying to deal

with you and all the pain you have caused me, and I could be working on much more productive things in therapy, things that benefit me, not this crap that is all about you. I have endured so much stress over this, I can't even tell you. It has consumed my waking hours and I don't even get any relief when I go to sleep because you visit me in my effing dreams, and I wake up and before I know it I am thinking about you again and again. I have not been able to do any work and my rent is due in three days and I don't have the money because I have missed two deadlines – something, as you know, I have taken pride in not having done in my whole professional career. I am widely known by all my clients as someone who is trustworthy and reliable, and I take great pride in these characteristics. And you have made me break that lifelong pattern. I have let people down, and I have let myself down, and you are off with Daylene and you are not taking responsibility for the breadth of the harm you are causing. So. I anticipate that I will be over you in approximately four weeks. I already get a discounted fee of $80 from my therapist, and I am willing to pay for half of it. As I said, I have already put six weeks into this, so that is ten weeks at $80 per hour, or $800. I would like to leave the end date open, but I would like, at least, to agree on $400 from you to start.

9.   I know that I can't ask you to move, even though I don't think I should have to bump into you and Daylene. Even if I don't see you, or one of your pseudo-intellectual, pretentious, underemployed "friends," I shouldn't have to stress out about it and worry and look around. I would like you to try to consolidate your errands so I can at least organize

my day in a peaceful way. And if you want to leave for a while, I think that it would be generous of you, to give me a break. I know that you are not a generous person, although you can be when you choose to, and I would ask that you look into your core and try to remember when you used to care for me and be nice to me and try to remember what those feelings felt like, and tap into those feelings, and think about leaving town for a while.

10.   I will be in downtown San Encanto on Wednesday at three p.m., with Niffy, for a Reiki appointment. I would like to pick up my stuff from you then, and I would appreciate it if you would be there to help me load my car. Part of me does not want to see you and I know that it will upset me to see you and have things be so different between us, and I know that it is in my best interest to stay away from you completely, but I don't think that I should have to load everything into my car by myself, especially if you are going to let me have the exercise ball. It is not heavy but it is cumbersome, and since I will have the dog, it will take some arranging in the car. I would appreciate it, and I know this goes without saying but I will say it anyway, and that is that I would appreciate it if Daylene was not there. I do not need to see her smug face, especially during this painful time. She is not a sensitive person. I don't know what you see in her. Clearly she has certain gifts that are obvious to the outsider, but I mean in terms of what kind of person she is, I don't think she is a good person and I don't respect her values. I know you don't care what I think. But anyone who does not respect the boundaries of another person's relationship has a moral structure that I think is

questionable and frankly, I think you should question it. If she screws me, so to speak, she will probably screw you later. She will hurt you and even though we are not in a relationship anymore, I still care about you and I would not feel comfortable if I did not warn you about her.

11. I will have been at the Reiki appointment for a good part of the morning and Niffy will be a bit stir crazy and I will need to walk her before I drive home, so if you want to take a walk when I get there to talk about things, I would be open to that. I will need to take a walk then anyway. You are welcome to come.

12. You have left some things at my house as well. I will bring them. There is your anorak jacket, which I'm sure you have been wanting. I hung it up, though you left it on the floor, and I can bring it over on Wednesday. I also have: your Radiohead CD, your chili cookbook, and your white tee shirt that you gave me to sleep in. I would like to keep the tee shirt. It is a light cotton and I have gotten used to sleeping with that weight. I will give it back to you if you want. I also have the stuffed Shamu that you won at SeaWorld. I assume that he was a gift for me, but I am learning, slowly, that I can't make any assumptions with you. Please let me know if you want Shamu back or if he is mine to keep.

13. If Wednesday is not convenient for you, it's fine with me if you bring my things over to my house. We can do a hand-off and you can pick up your things here and drop mine off. I will be at work during the day, of course, but if you want to come by in the evening, that is fine. I have plans

for various nights, but let me know what evening works for you and I will let you know if I am here, or can arrange to be so. I would like to work this out in a peaceful way, so I am willing to be flexible.

14.   If it will smooth things over for me to say it, then all right, I'm sorry for "hitting" Daylene with the car. I barely made contact with her and honestly I'm not sure the car even touched her. The whole "falling down" thing was totally over the top on her part. We both know that I was just trying to get her to move so I could leave with some degree of dignity intact. But I am willing to meet you halfway, so if it helps for me to say it then I will say it (to you, not to her): I'm sorry.

15.   When you stop by with my things, I would appreciate it if you would block out some time to talk to me. I think that if you just came here and dropped off my stuff it would be very upsetting and I would like to process it a little with you before you just leave to go be with Daylene again. I am not asking for a marriage proposal, so please don't take it that way. Believe me, that is the last thing that I want from you. I want to move on. But I would like to talk with you, calmly, and I think that it would help me to process what you did to me and perhaps shorten the amount of time that I have to spend processing it in therapy, so if you look at it from a financial standpoint, it would be the most cost-effective approach for both of us. I am free on Thursday after eight or Friday after seven. I would like to see you and talk to you and I know that it is over between us and I am fine with that, I am glad about that, but we had

something that was very important to me and I believe
that it was important to you, too, even though you threw it
away. Please let me know what you would like to do.

— Spirit

SAFEKEEPING

"We're much more than a storage company," I say.

This is how they make us answer the phone. Half the time it leaves people speechless. This time when I answer the phone, the caller starts to snicker. "What else are you?" he says.

"Excuse me?"

"If you're more than a storage company, what else are you?" He sounds like a pissy history teacher.

"We're a storage company," I say. "We also offer personal service and twenty-four-hour security."

"Those are aspects of a storage company," he says. "Not additions. So really, you're just a storage company."

"That's correct," I say. "How can I help you?"

"You're quick to abandon your claim."

I don't answer. Omar, my manager, looks up from where he's stocking the air fresheners.

"Hello?" says the man, like I'm an idiot.

"Yes sir," I say. "Are you looking for a storage solution?"

"Yes, I am. I would hope so. Otherwise I'd be mighty stupid calling a storage facility."

I think of my mother pulling up at 5:15, her hands on the steering wheel, her eyes turned to me with expectation. I have no wish to tell her I got fired again.

"How can I help you?" I ask.

"You can tell me your name, for starters," he says.

"This is Abby," I tell him. "Abby Zinger."

"Well, Miss Zinger, I have equipment that's very valuable, worth thousands of dollars, and I don't feel confident that your facility can ensure their security based on my interaction with you thus far. So, I suggest you put your manager on the phone before I get even more frustrated and take my business elsewhere."

Omar is dumping coffee grounds from the urn in the waiting room into the trash. He brushes dark specks from the counter into his palm and then wipes his hands over the trash can. He picks up a blue shammy and peers around the whiteners for more dust.

"If you want to store your equipment here," I whisper into the phone, "do it. We're more than a storage company because I personally pee on one item in every storage locker at the end of every shift. I will pee on your belongings." My tone softens. "Do you want to talk to my manager now?"

There's nothing but silence on the other end of the phone. "Yes," the man says, but his voice is different. The air is gone from it. "Put him on."

I lower the phone, call Omar's name and gesture him over. "I think it's a crank call, but I'm not sure," I say with a helpless wince. "Will you talk to him for me?" He takes the phone with irritation.

"We're much more than a storage company," he says into the receiver. The room hangs in silence for a moment as we both don't move.

"We're much more than a storage company," he says again.

He hands me back the phone.

"Crank call," he says. "They hung up. We get those sometimes. People with nothing better to do."

"Thanks for handling it," I say to him. I take the dust shammy from his hand and smile with my eyes. "Let me do that for you."

At dusk my mom picks me up, and after asking how my day was, we drive home in a nagging silence. She starts to ask me a question at the same time that I lean forward and switch on the radio. We both stop and she looks embarrassed.

"What?" I say.

She offers a hesitant smile. "Nothing," she says. I wait for her to say more, but she doesn't.

When we get home I go into my room and throw myself across the bed. Faded neon stars glow down from the ceiling. My mom starts making dinner and the aroma of spaghetti sauce wafts through my bedroom door, left open per a new house rule. My dad is watching Peter Jennings talk about the Clinton impeachment hearings in the living room. I always know when a politician comes on the news because I can hear him talking back at the TV, telling whoever it is they are a shyster or a common idiot. Supposedly he was a gallivanting journalist when my parents met – their first date was the night that Skylab fell, they love to tell the story – but he quit to write travel guides when Ollie and I were little. Now he yells at Peter Jennings like it was his fault.

Down the hall and to the left, Ollie lies on his bed, too, practicing his magic tricks, flipping cards from hand to hand. I haven't seen my brother without a deck of cards since he was ten. At night, he works them in the dark underneath the covers. On weekends, he does magic shows with his best friend, Max, who lives next door. They perform in the driveway for our neighbors – Owen Appelbaum, a nebbishy guy who still lives with his mother three doors down; Kenneth, the cul-de-sac's resident Deadhead; or Alice,

Max's little sister. Sometimes they even get a birthday party gig.

At 6:30, the news is over and the spaghetti is ready so we sit around the table and eat, my parents with glasses of wine next to their plates and my brother with a deck of cards next to his.

"How's your new job?" my dad asks me. A drop of red sauce flies onto his white shirt as he twirls spaghetti.

"I don't mind it. It's not hard."

"You want a job to be hard," he says. "If it's not hard, you're not learning anything. You're spinning your wheels."

"She's learning how to keep a job," my mom says. "That's worth something."

"Millions of people can say that, Betty," my father answers. "Literally billions." My parents take turns being angry and depressed like it's on a chore wheel taped to the fridge. Tonight my mom chews her lip and stares at my dad, who seems to miss the whole performance. Then he turns to me. "Don't sell yourself short. That's all I'm saying."

"I won't," I tell him. "Can I get a Coke?"

"You know, it's not too late to register for classes in the Spring," he says as I push my chair away from the table. His voice rises as I walk into the kitchen. "Your mother and I have college degrees, and there's no reason you shouldn't have one, too."

I open the refrigerator and peer at the yogurt and string cheese and apple juice. I can hear my brother in the other room, flipping the cards in his hand. "Watch this one," he's saying.

"We know this one, honey," my mom says. "Not at the table."

"I just invented it. This one is new," he says. I find a Coke in the back, behind a carton of milk. "Wait," Ollie is saying. "Let me do it again. Just watch." The cards rustle in his hands.

My mother drops me off at the storage company the next day. I have one hand on the passenger-side door about to open it when she speaks. "If you want to talk to someone," she says, as if I'm catching her mid-sentence, "like a psychiatrist, I mean." I let go of the handle. "If you want to, your father and I would pay for it."

My chest crackles and I catch my breath.

"Or, are you feeling better now?" she continues quickly. That look flashes across her face, like a dog that loves its master, even as it readies to be kicked.

"I'm fine, Mom," I say, getting out of the car. "Everything is fine."

I walk up to the office and hear the car pull away from the curb. The storage facility is gray, with its name in big orange plastic letters stuck on the roof, and orange metal doors on all the storage spaces that line the parking lot. There are more units inside. The interior ones just have regular orange doors, not the pull-down kind, and sometimes when I walk the hallways I hear my shoes squeak on the flooring and imagine that behind each door is an inmate locked in solitary confinement. I jingle the keys in my pocket. The building sits on the corner of a frontage road and a potholed industrial street, but if you keep driving for about six blocks, shops start to appear and then an elementary school, where a grandmotherly-looking crossing guard always waits on the corner with her stop sign, looking official. Sometimes we wave to each other as my mom and I drive past.

When I walk inside, Omar is sitting at his desk in the back corner, squinting at his computer screen. He bounces his knee with a restless energy he always seems to have. I think he would jump around the office on a pogo stick if he could. His blue shirt hangs loosely on his muscular shoulders as his leg moves up and down. He raises his head when I come in.

"Good morning," he says. "I looked over your inventory sheets from last night. You forgot to record the new client receipts."

"Oh," I say, putting down my bag slowly and thoughtfully. "Sorry about that. I can do it right now if you want."

"I already did it," he says. "We have to send those numbers to headquarters on Wednesdays. You need to check your work against the list before you go home," he says, turning in his swivel chair to face me. "You have to check your work every day."

"Okay," I say. "I thought I did that. I'll make sure to check it from now on." I pull the laminated card from under the desk blotter and pretend to read it. I stare at it until I feel him turn in his chair and stop watching me.

The first three hours pass slowly. We have two new walk-in customers and one man with an Iron Maiden tee shirt who says he has forgotten the combination to his locker. Omar leaps up and takes him back to his desk, where they sit and speak quietly while Omar fills out the man's answers to a complex questionnaire on a clipboard. It isn't enough just to show your photo ID. You have to verify bank numbers and passwords and the date you opened the account. Omar reluctantly gives the man a new combination and walks with him back toward the maze of hallways.

I am about to leave on my lunch break when the phone rings. "We're much more than a storage company," I say.

There is a quick beat of silence and then a man speaks. "Yes," he says. "I want to rent a storage locker. I want to know your rates."

"It depends on the size of the locker and how long you rent it for," I say. "How much stuff do you have?"

"Oh, I don't know," he says liltingly. "A bit of this, a bit of that. The detritus of life one can't part with."

I wait for him to go on. "Well," I say, "the first month is free no matter what. Then you can get anything from a large locker for $15 a month to a whole garage for $200. The prices go down if you buy them for more than six months at a time."

"Lovely," the man says. "I may do that. I may come down. Would it be all right if I came down and had a look?"

"Sure," I say. "We're open until midnight."

"But you won't be there until midnight, will you?" He laughs.

It's that crank caller from yesterday. I hang up.

I stare at the phone and wait for it to ring again. Omar comes out a few minutes later without the customer, who's probably sitting on the floor sifting through his old electric bills now. I pick up the shammy and dust the ficus in the waiting room, glancing out the glass doors and into the front parking lot. It's empty.

At home that night, we all watch *Ally McBeal.* My dad sits in the recliner with his eyes closed while my mom curls on the sofa under a blanket. She reaches for her Benzedrex on the side table and absently inhales in each nostril. My brother sits on the rug and cuts his cards with one hand.

My dad checks his watch, puts both hands on his knees and says, "I'm gonna head over to Jack's 665."

My mom looks bewildered. "It's nine o'clock, Robert," she says.

"There's still time to play a few hands." He gets his coat from the closet. "I won't be long." We hear the engine whine as he pulls out. My mom stares at the door like there's still a conversation to be had, like he didn't just disappear. *Poof.*

Ollie shuffles his cards. "Can you give it a rest, Ollie?" I say. I stand up and step over him. He stops.

"Where are you going?" my mother asks.

"My room," I say. I go down the hall and lie across my bed. I look up at the glow-in-the-dark stars and think about the man who called me. I wonder if he really is going to "come in and have a look." I wonder if I'll know him when he does.

The rest of the week is quiet. On Thursday two women come in to stash a bunch of stuff for one of them, who is going to live abroad for a year. They're both teary-eyed as they unload a bicycle, boxes of dishes and books, and a yellow bean bag chair. "You can't store paint in here," I tell them when they come out. I saw them unload it on the video feed. For a minute the shorter one looks panicked, but her friend gives her arm a squeeze.

"It's okay, you can leave it at my house," she says. She shoots me a look over her shoulder as they walk back into the tangle of hallways.

Other than that, we only have a few regulars – hoarders who need to touch their piles of litter every few days or else they become anxious, and small business owners who use the units to store all their paperwork in case their houses blow up or fall down. I make the coffee and throw out the grounds and tally the client receipts and water the ficus. Omar keeps mostly to himself at his desk in the back. I begin to enjoy the repetition of my days – the sweep of a hand over coffee dust; the chemical smell of the flat blue carpet; the quiet hum of the computer; the rectangles of sunlight that move across the waiting room floor as the day presses forward. I have my desk, or my spot behind the counter anyway, and it is my domain. I straighten out the stack of brochures beside me.

At three o'clock, the bells chime and a man walks through the door, silhouetted by the glare. He approaches the counter steadily, his shoes silent as he places them along the carpet. Slowly my eyes adjust and I can see his face. He's in his fifties, with a ruddy complexion and tortoiseshell glasses. His reddish hair has a soft wave to it and his eyebrows are a little bit wild. He wears a green windbreaker and a crumpled button-down shirt underneath. When he reaches the counter he grasps the edge lightly with his fingertips. His hands are bony and dry. His mouth curls at the edges into a smile.

"Hello," he says in a familiar, lilting tone. "I'd like to rent a storage unit."

It's the guy. I can't take my eyes off him. "Okay," I say. "What size do you want? You can see what we have in the brochure."

He glances at the pamphlets but doesn't pick one up. "I don't need anything too big," he says. His voice is smooth and controlled. "Perhaps the size of a large walk-in closet. Can you show me what you have that might look like that?"

Omar taps away at a spreadsheet at his desk. He doesn't look up.

"The dimensions are all in the brochure," I say.

"I'm sure they are," he says. "And I'll take one of these to look at when I get home. But I'm more of a visual person. I need to see the space to know if it will suit my needs."

"Fine," I say. I pick up a clipboard that lists the vacant units and walk around the counter. "Follow me."

We walk down the hallway lined with orange doors, my imaginary inmates silent as we pass their cells. He keeps a few paces behind me and doesn't say anything. I stop when we get to an empty unit, unlock the door and stand aside. He peers around the doorframe and into the stale room.

"Do the rooms stay dry?" he asks.

"The units are all above ground, and there isn't a sprinkler system. You won't get any water damage."

"No sprinkler system?" he says. "What if there's a fire?"

"The doors are metal. Fire can't get through them. It's safer than sprinklers."

He peers again inside the room.

"Are the units climate controlled?" he asks.

"The indoor ones are. The drive-up units aren't. The indoor units are always between fifty-five and seventy-five degrees."

"Good, good," he says. He turns and faces me. "I collect old clocks, some as many as a hundred years old. The wood and interior parts are very sensitive."

I nod. "Well, like I said, the indoor units are climate controlled. They cost a little bit extra."

"Of course." He steps away from the doorway. "This will be fine, thank you."

I close the door and lock it. "There are some disclosure forms for you to fill out up front," I say.

"What kind of disclosures?" he asks with a laugh in his throat, as if this is something funny.

We start walking back down the hallway. "There's a compliance sheet that you sign. You have to promise not to store any stolen or toxic items. You can't live there." I open the main door back to the front. "You can't keep anything dangerous inside."

We walk into the lobby. I go behind the counter and hand him the forms. He takes the papers with his bony fingers. I look over the sheets when he is done filling them out and run his credit card.

"We have a dolly you can use if you need it. And if you come after eight p.m., you need to enter a key code at the front gate. The code is on your contract." I point to it.

"It won't be after eight," he says. "Thank you for your time." He takes the yellow and pink copies of his contract and walks out the glass door into the parking lot, the little bells chiming as he leaves.

Omar comes out of the bathroom, wiping his hands on his khaki pants. He looks embarrassed when he sees me. He walks

quickly to his desk and starts tapping at his computer. I sit and
stare at the speckled brown counter that is my workspace. The For-
mica siding is coming off where the glue is old and dry, and the
desk blotter smells like mildew. Some administrative assistant who
came before me has drawn little stars all around the sides of it in
pencil. I rub my finger over one of them, and the charcoal color
comes off onto my fingertip.

"I have to make a deposit at the bank now," Omar says, standing up and lifting his coat off the coat rack. He shrugs it onto his
shoulders, then picks up a blue plastic envelope with the week's
receipts. "I'll be back in an hour or two."

"I'm off in an hour and a half," I say, glancing at the clock.

"I'll be back by then," he says. The bells tinkle behind him. Then
the office is completely quiet. I sit without moving until I become
aware of the rise and fall of my chest and the air coming in and
out of my nose. The phone doesn't ring and no one comes in. I can
hear the faint rush of cars every few minutes as they drive by on the
frontage road. I take out a piece of paper and draw a line down the
middle. On one side I write "PRO," and on the other side I write
"CON." I can't think of anything to fill in on either side, so I throw
the paper away.

At 4:30, a brown sedan pulls into the parking lot. The man
is back with his "detritus." He looks straight ahead as he drives
toward the back entrance. His car and everything in it jostles as he
goes over the speed bump without slowing down. I watch him until
he drives into the south lot, and I can't see him anymore.

After a few minutes, he shows up on the video monitor. He
carries a suitcase in one hand and a shopping bag in the other,
and he pushes a cockeyed box down the hallway with his foot. He
stops in front of his unit and unlocks it. He props open the door

and heaves the suitcase in. The image on the monitor is black and white and it skitters and bends toward the left on top, but I can still make out what he is doing. He leaves the door propped open and makes trip after trip from his car to the unit, bringing in more tattered boxes, an old hi-fi, some speakers, and what looks like a cat scratcher. He brings in a couple of old clocks, just like he said he would, and when he does, he carries those in separately, holding each one delicately in front of him like a birthday cake. He comes in again awkwardly carrying an ironing board pressed between his left arm and his side. In his right hand, he holds a gun.

I blink a few times to be sure, but nothing changes. It looks like a big revolver, something you might see on John Wayne or Clint Eastwood. I turn around to Omar's desk and then remember he has gone to the bank. I watch the man on the monitor. I know it sounds weird, but it makes me furious. *You think I'm afraid of you?* I think. I press myself up from my chair, muscles buzzing. I walk to the back of the lobby and pull open the heavy metal door to the interior units. My feet squeak along the cement floor as I stride down the white-painted cinderblock halls, orange metal doors punctuating my way one after the other.

"Hey!" I call out as soon as I round his corner. I grip my keys in my hand. He looks up at me with surprise. "You can't keep firearms here," I say when I get up to his face. He puts the ironing board down with a grunt. He looks at the gun in his hand.

"This old thing?" he says. "This is a relic. It doesn't even fire any-more." He waves it around as if to show its harmlessness.

"It doesn't matter," I say. "It was in the paperwork I showed you. You can't keep any weapons or ammunition here. I told you that this afternoon."

"I don't think you heard what I just told you," he says. "This isn't a working gun. It's a worthless piece of metal."

"If it's worthless, then what are you keeping it for?" I ask him. I am so tired of people never saying what they mean.

He stiffens and grips the gun tighter, casting it around as he talks. "It's worthless in terms of its usage, but it's not worthless to me. I shouldn't have to explain to you the concept of *value*." He seethes when he says this last part.

"If it's so valuable," I say, "then put it under your pillow and keep it at your house."

"I'm not going to keep it at my house," he says. He takes a step toward me and the scent of musky aftershave breathes off his neck and goes down my throat. "I'm going to keep it here, at this storage facility, where I have just paid you a three-month deposit. This is now my unit, and I will use it as I see fit."

"Fine," I say. "I'm calling the police." I turn to walk back to the office.

I take three steps.

"Don't," he says.

I stop, slowly pivot and face him.

"The gun is not reliable, all right? It jams. I can't keep it at my house."

"Why not?" I ask.

He waits a moment. "I just can't."

"You said it doesn't fire."

He shifts. "I can't have it around my wife, all right?"

I flex my fingers, damp around the keys.

"It's a matter of personal safety."

An awareness tickles at my mind. "Why?" I ask him. "Did your wife try to off you?"

"No," he says. His shoulders settle underneath his green jacket.

"Herself."

The man suddenly looks old. Everything about him looks old: his faded jeans, worn at the cuffs; his smudged eyeglasses; the curling hairs of his eyebrows, peppered with gray.

"There are lots of ways to kill yourself, you know," I tell him. "You don't need a gun to do it."

We stand there facing each other, he with the gun in his hand, me with the keys in mine.

"Just don't leave it in the open," I say quietly. "Put it under a pile of stuff."

"Thank you," he says, relieved. He walks into the unit, lifts a folded blanket and slips the gun underneath. Then he looks over his shoulder at me. "You're not going to pee on it, are you?"

"What? No," I say, startled. "We don't do that here."

"Thank goodness," he says.

Back at the front desk, I watch him unload the rest of his junk on the video monitor. After about thirty minutes, I see him drive out through the parking gate, his small head bobbing as he goes over the speed bump, passing Omar as he drives in.

Later that evening, my mom is cooking chicken cacciatore in the kitchen. I can hear my dad watching Peter Jennings on TV. I pass my brother's doorway as I make my way to my room. He sits on his bed fanning the deck of cards along his forearm. He glances up at me and back at his cards as I walk by. "Hi," he says.

"Hi, Ollie," I say back, and then stop and walk into his room. "What are you doing?" I ask him. His eyes become animated.

"I made up a new trick," he says. "Do you want to see it?"

"Yeah, sure," I say. I sit on the bed next to him.

"It's called 'The Deluge.'" He draws his hands apart like

a conductor, the cards flowing between them like an ocean wave.

"Wow," I say. "That's a great trick."

He chortles. "That's not even a trick," he says dismissively. "That's called a flourish." He shuffles the cards a few more times and then flicks his hand and the cards spread out before me. "Pick a card, any card."

I do.

"Now put it back in the middle."

He flips the deck into four sections and pivots them through his fingers. He weaves and spins the cards. Then he snaps his fingers. My card rises up from the middle, peeking at me like a Vegas sunrise.

"That's fantastic," I tell him. His eyes glisten.

I get up and go toward my room, stopping in the kitchen doorway to watch my mother from behind. She bends at the counter, her hands dredging poultry in white flour. She presses each piece with her thumbs, making a much harder go of it than she has to. I think of her, coming to pick me up at 5:15 every day, her neck craning forward as she drives. Always in anticipation, trying to head off whatever blow life has in store, whatever ambush lies in wait. Especially from me.

I reach around her to get a Coke and she jumps, startled by my shadow.

"You scared me," she says. She puts her hand on her chest as if to slow her beating heart.

"I know," I tell her. I open up the Coke and take a sip. "I'm sorry."

I lean against the counter next to her, and we don't say anything until it's time for dinner.

ALICE

It was the summer the worm grew out of Alice's stomach. It was my job to worry it out, bit by bit. Every day I twirled a little bit more around a slender, bleached stick that the doctor had given to our mother. Alice cried every night as I coaxed out the oily crawler, more than two feet in all, from her overburdened intestine.

Even in suburbia they still work worms out the old way, just like they do in the remote village where she contracted the thing. We had stayed in nice hotels and never left the tour bus, but Alice was a wanderer. My dad used to joke that he would put her on a leash if the neighbors weren't so judgmental. Alice was eight that summer. I was eleven.

As her older brother, it was my job to watch her. Make sure she didn't roam into an uncovered swimming pool, poke a barbed wire fence. A curious girl, she could be drawn to play in a garbage dump the way a cartoon character might be lured by the aroma of baking bread. Always lifting things up, running her fingers along the jagged edge of a can after it had been opened.

One day, she wandered away from the tour bus, for only ten or twenty minutes. I found her out behind the picnic site, squatting in a mud puddle, drawing her hand across her reflection and talking in a sing-song voice. I led her back to the group.

They say the worm egg probably hatched that winter. It grew into the spring, nestled in her abdomen, sleeping through its adolescence, not yet ready to emerge. When it did, it started out as a sore just below her belly button. A bump. Then a blister. It hurt, she said. It got nastier, red and ugly, bulbous and full of pus. We thought it was an infected pimple, or a boil. My mother put ointment on it, white cream that turned clear when she rubbed it in. "Alice Pippick," Mom would say, "your picking at it isn't doing you any good." Alice was miserable. The worm inside continued to grow.

Alice did pick at it, Mom was right. And one day, as the air got warmer and the days got longer, she dabbed and pressed and squeezed and the worm popped its wary head out. She showed me in our bedroom and we watched it pulse. Alice developed a fever. We drove to the hospital.

Guinea worm, the doctor said. He brought in interns and residents and they all took a look at Alice. They photographed her seated, lying down, standing left, standing right. They gave my mother the stick, a narrow little tongue depressor, and told us to turn the stick just so, softly, evenly, or the worm could break in two. "It could take weeks," they told us. "Maybe months."

In the car, my mother gave the stick to me. She couldn't bring herself to do it. Besides, she said, I had a steadier hand.

We got drive-thru on the way home. Alice wasn't hungry. She lay down in the back seat, gently holding her belly, still thick with baby fat, and now with something else.

She lay sleeping, a little lump under the covers. Alice had lined her teddy bears and stuffed dog up against the wall, instead of clutching them like she used to. I knew it was because she didn't want them to touch the worm. Not because she thought they would bump the thing; it was secure under its bandages. But because she didn't want them to be near it, to be contaminated by its watery oil. I put my hand on her shoulder.

"Come on, Bug. I have to twirl Alfie."

I had taken to calling the worm Alfie, trying to make him more like a friend.

"Don't wanna," she muttered, eyes still closed.

"The sooner we do it, the sooner we get it done. Come on, roll over."

She stayed still for a minute while I stood above her, and then slowly rolled onto her back. She lifted up her shirt. "Good girl," I said. I took the corner of the white medical tape and slowly began pulling it off of her skin. She held onto my wrist. The tape tugged at her as it came up. She clenched her eyes against tears.

Alfie straightened up as if to greet me. As I turned the stick he curled around it, gripping it gently, making my job easier. I wondered if he knew that the end of this process would be the end of his life.

I rolled the stick in my hand.

The sun rose early that summer and burned high all day. Alice couldn't run for fear of falling down; she couldn't play tag and risk getting jostled. The cul-de-sac was deserted, so Alice and I went to the creek to look for salamanders. We played tetherball in the yard. We lay down on the wet grass after the sprinklers finished, trying to hide from the heat.

Over time, she didn't cry anymore when I did it.

Dad left for work first, while we were still in bed. We were up, in the living room, while Mom pulled herself together. I lay on my stomach reading a *Peanuts* comic. Charlie Brown was falling for the old football trick again. Mom's feet paced from room to room as she gathered her handbag, her keys, her sunglasses. She turned to us. "Be good, Alice. You too, Max," she said. The light streamed in as she opened the door, and when she closed it behind her the air sucked out of the room and followed her like a vacuum, a whispered whoosh.

I lay there for a minute on the carpet, the beige strands spreading out before me like wheat. Alice stared at me from her spot on the floor next to the ottoman, then she brought her attention back down to the coloring book before her. She dragged a blue crayon in broad strokes across the cartoon sky.

We sat in the driveway. Alice brought out her jacks and bounced the rubber ball, swiping her hand underneath and gathering the little pronged men as she told herself a story under her breath. Long as a finger now, Alfie lay coiled against her stomach, sleeping under gauze and strips of white tape. I leaned back on my hands and looked up at the sky. Broad swashes of clouds painted themselves against the bright blue backdrop. I looked for faces in the clouds. The sky was flat, a tray with a thousand cotton balls on it, all in sweeping patterns. And then, below the cotton, below the curving paths of blurry, white balls, I saw it: a blimp. Drifting weightlessly, coolly, silently. In the glare it looked like a big round man and it made me want to laugh.

"What are we going to do now, Max?" said Alice.

"What?" I said. She slouched over her game, having drawn all the entertainment there was to be extracted from it. She waited.

She licked her lips from the heat. I sat up. A tiny pebble dug into my palm. I looked back at the sky and tried to see which way the clouds were moving, but they stayed where they were, fixed. I tried to find the blimp-man again, but he was gone.

Alice was on the couch with one arm on her stomach and the other hanging over the side when our father came home from work. I sat in the big chair on the opposite side of the room. We were watching an old black and white Popeye cartoon while my mother prepared dinner in the kitchen. He leaned his head into the den.

"Hey kids," he said.

"Hi," we answered.

"How ya doing?" he asked.

"Good."

"Whatcha watching?"

"Popeye," said Alice, rolling her eyes and stating the obvious.

"Oh, okay, sorry Missy. Pardon me. I didn't mean to intrude on your TV time."

He turned to leave and I stopped him. "Hey, Dad," I said.

"What's up, son?"

"Remember how you said I could have my own room soon?"

He gave me a smile, then wrinkled his nose. "Yeah. We have to work that out. If we don't have a guest room, where's Grandma going to stay when she visits?"

"She can sleep in my room," I said. "Besides, Grandma hasn't been here in two years."

"I'll talk about it with your mother," Dad said. "We know you want it, son. We hear you loud and clear."

He disappeared from the doorway and I heard him greet my mother in the kitchen, heard the conversation pause for a kiss between them, and then continue in hushed voices, punctuated by an occasional echo of laughter. On TV, Bluto had slung Olive

Oyl over his shoulder and was striding off with her as she pounded against his back.

I stood in front of the bathroom mirror. I swished mouth-wash around, gurgling it in my throat. I tilted my chin down and pumped it between my teeth. I held it there, suspended. I spit. My hair hung over my forehead, falling into four sections. To me they looked like little soldiers, standing guard, standing by. On the ready, sir. At your command. I touched the scars on my face that ran from my cheek to my lip.

"Ready, Bug?" I called. Alice didn't answer. I turned and went into the bedroom.

Alice lay curled on the bed in a tangled sheet. The room was still hot and stuffy from the afternoon sun, even though now it was night. She watched as I walked over and sat down on her bed.

She turned and faced the wall and mouthed words to her stuffed animals.

"Don't be mad at me about this," I said, but before I got all the words out she answered in a voice even louder, "I'm not mad at you about this."

"You sound mad," I said, and again she answered, "I'm not mad," before I was finished.

"Roll over, then," I said.

She didn't move. I turned her shoulder down against the mat-tress. She craned her head up toward the wall.

"Relax," I said. "Will you relax?"

I uncovered the gauze and turned the stick, but the worm wouldn't budge.

"He won't come out tonight," I said. I leaned over her, awkwardly grasping for the right angle.

"Turn on the light," said Alice.

"I don't need the light," I said. "Will you let me do my job?"

I got on top of her.

He didn't move at first, and then he did, just a tremble on the end.

"I got it now," I said.

Alice stared at me. We faced each other in the moonlit room as I rolled the stick and wound the worm around it. Alfie strained, turning pale where he was taut, resisted. He stretched long as I pulled, clinging to Alice's tissues inside, where he had been so long embedded. I pressed her shoulder down and turned, slow and steady, turned.

Alice's animals watched me, blank-eyed gawkers.

Then it was over. I let go of the stick. He was out more now, another quarter inch. Alice's small hand still gripped my forearm. I lay the gauze back on and pressed down strips of clean white tape. I thought: In a few weeks this will all be over. Alfie will be dead, and we can get on with our lives. I stroked the hair from Alice's forehead. Her chest rose and fell. Her gaze remained on me, steady.

"That's my Bug," I said gently. "My good Bug."

THE ACORN

At lunchtime Hannah comes up behind me at my cubicle and says, "Hey, Owen. Wanna go to Tortola?" I minimize my Solitaire game. The cursor glimmers. I swivel around and even though she has said my name, for a moment I'm not sure if she's talking to me. She stands there, her nostrils gently pulsing. I'm about to speak when Fergus and Daylene hustle up and ask her if she wants to go to Snagwiches.

My phone rings. It's Mother.

Do I want to have meatloaf for dinner, she asks. Mother's meatloaf is nothing but meat and onions and ketchup. No bread crumbs mushing it down. Yes, I tell her. I want to have meatloaf for dinner.

I look up. Hannah and her hangers-on are a hive of jackets disappearing through the door.

Later, when I'm shutting down my computer, Hannah comes back to my cubicle and slides down onto the floor. "I got dumped last night," she says. A strange feeling grips my innards.

"I'm sorry," I say. "I didn't even know you were seeing someone."

"It was Andrew Bang, from tech support," she says. She opens her purse and flips through it, then closes it without retrieving anything. "He said he still had feelings for Elaine Panopolis in HR."

"Wow," I say. "Elaine Panopolis."

"Do you know her?" she asks.

"I've seen her around." Elaine Panopolis has mousy brown hair and ankles that are so wide strangers notice them. "Were you in love with him?" I ask, and then I stop breathing.

"Yeah, I guess so," Hannah says. "I said I was. He said it back."

I exhale and decide to go for broke, just lunge after my basest urges. I ask her if she wants to get a drink to drown her sorrows. I say it with a touch of glibness and a chaser of whimsy, and wave my ballpoint pen like it's Groucho Marx's cigar for some reason. But the janitor turns on his industrial strength vacuum the moment I open my mouth, and I just sit there flapping my pen and grinning, drowned out by the roar. Hannah stands up and brushes carpet lint from her skirt. The janitor moves down the aisle.

"Well," Hannah says, "such is life. Have a good night, Owen." She takes two steps toward me and leans forward, bending at the waist. Then she runs her thumb along my right eyebrow, smoothing it down. "These are long," she says. "Bye bye."

"Goodbye," I say. My voice feels tacky in my mouth, and she opens the security doors to the elevators and is gone.

That evening, I hop off my bike and onto the sidewalk in front of my house. The air is cool and I can smell the meatloaf in the oven as soon as I walk in the door. I used to be embarrassed that I still lived at home even though I'm just north of thirty, but since my mom has gotten older, instead of saying I live with her, now I say she lives with me. The truth is, I did move out in my twenties but my mother kept having what she thought were heart attacks and getting carted off in ambulances, and even though they couldn't find anything wrong with her, I just moved back home.

The meatloaf is everything I want it to be, and after dinner we settle down for a game of Scrabble, like usual. She leans back in her chair so far I think she'll tip over trying to read the letters on her tiles.

"When are you going to get new glasses?" I ask her.

"I can see just fine," she says. "Why should I give $200 to some chiseler when I can get a perfectly good pair of reading glasses at Walgreens for five dollars?" She teeters on the chair's back legs and grabs the table for balance.

"Ah ha," she says slowly. She smiles at her tray. Then with a shaky hand, she lays down JAKAZIN. "10... 18... 27... double word score, 54 points!"

"What does that mean?" I ask.

"It's some kind of spice, I think. Or a vein."

"I challenge you."

"Go ahead," she says defiantly. I stand up to get the dictionary and her eyes follow me, like a child after they deny they've broken the cookie jar but before you find the crumbs in their bed. "Wait," she says.

I sit back down.

"It's a vein. I'm sure of it."

Her lower lip quivers in a way that it's been doing lately, a tic she brushes off when I ask her about it.

I decide to let it go. "If you're sure you're sure," I say.

"I'm sure."

Though she'd never admit it, the wins mean more to her than they do to me. She hardly ever leaves the house anymore. She used to play bingo with her girlfriends but two of them died and one moved to Florida and she's lost interest in most everything else. She just wants to have dinner with me, hear about my job and tell me how to do it better. I don't mind. I tell her she should get a hobby but she says, "I've had a hobby for the past thirty-one years," and she means me.

She quit working when I was born. My dad had a heart attack and died when I was eight, and after that my mom started volunteering at my elementary school. She only wanted to work in my classes, though, and the teachers didn't like her. When they'd correct my answers in multiplication or adjust my form in cursive, Mother would whisper, "Don't listen to her. If she knew what she was doing she wouldn't be lording her talents over a bunch of *children*." No one could stop her. Even in PE, she would stand at the sidelines during dodgeball games and shriek, "On your left!" I never took a hit. Finally the other kids complained and the school said they didn't need her to help out anymore.

I play WAY for eleven points when I could have played WAIVER for twenty-seven. She smiles to herself and nestles down into her chair.

I work at a place called Inspirvation!, which makes inspirational and motivational posters. The next day I'm eating a burrito at my desk when Wally Nortweller comes up behind me and holds out a new protocol. "I need you to start following this rubric," he says. "I've established metrics to incent you to make your outputs more robust."

Wally used to be my teammate but now he's my manager, and he keeps thinking of new protocols and drawing them up in Venn diagrams. I glance at the handout. This one has three overlapping circles: Customers, Outreach, and "Panthers," which is what he has decided to name our team, which used to be called Internal Support and Information Distribution. The little space where the circles intersect is labeled "The Future."

"What about the M-Power Protocol?" I ask him.

"This one supersedes that. We'll be meeting about it on Friday, but I need you to be intimate with its methodologies before then. It's our number one priority."

He leans in front of me and places the paper on my desk. A tuft of dandruff blossoms in his ear. I move my burrito to the side. It's gone clammy, anyway.

I open up an interoffice chat window and type Hannah's name. "Have you seen the new proto..." My phone rings. I check the caller ID. It's Mother.

It's not my mother, though. It's our neighbor, Midge Pippick, calling from my mother's line. I don't remember the words she says, I only remember looking at the rice grains in my burrito as I hear her say them. Black bean sauce soaks through and they bloat under its weight. It's the loneliest thing my eyes have ever seen.

When I get to the house half an hour later, yellow police tape blocks the front door. I toss my bike onto the lawn and tear the tape down as I rush inside. Just one cop is there, a woman, sitting at my kitchen table filling out forms on a clipboard. She looks up when I come in.

"You're not supposed to be in here until I clear the scene," she says.

"I live here," I say. "My name is Owen Appelbaum. The woman who lives here is my mother."

"I'm sorry for your loss," the policewoman says. Her automatic pencil tip snaps as she darkens a checkbox on her form.

"Why is there crime scene tape up?" I ask. "Did somebody hurt her?"

The woman clicks her pencil until more lead comes out. "No, she choked on a piece of candy. I just put the tape up so I can finish these forms. I always keep some around. You'd be surprised."

"Oh, dear," I hear Midge say from behind me. "I'm so sorry, honey." She reaches out a hand but I just stand there, so she drops her arm to her side. "You should have seen all the emergency vehicles," she says. "Your mother called 911 but they got here too late. They couldn't understand her with all of the gurgling."

I look at the phone on the wall next to the kitchen counter, still and quiet. I feel the hard candy lodged in my mother's throat.

"There was a fire truck and an ambulance and several police cars. Two fire trucks, actually," Midge says. "I was trying to take a nap. I've been so tired lately with the time change."

"Okay, hon," the lady cop says. She tears off a white sheet and hands me a yellow one. The tracings of her notes are indecipherable on my copy. "The number at the bottom is the San Encanto coroner. Give him a day or so, though. We're backed up."

She passes Midge in the doorway and walks into the front yard, where she turns and calls over her shoulder, "This your bike?"

"Yes," I say.

"Okay," she answers.

Midge rocks on her heels for a minute and then says, "If there's anything you need."

She closes the door behind her. I stand in the kitchen and listen to the deep hum of the refrigerator. I scratch a bug bite on my shoulder.

The coroner's office tells me I can retrieve her body or they can deliver it to the resting place of my choice for an extra fee. I spend some time googling cemeteries and decide on one in Colma where

Joe DiMaggio is buried. It gets a lot of direct sunlight and there's a windswept sycamore tree in the picture. I don't see the tree when we have the actual funeral, and the noise from the highway makes it hard to hear what the rabbi is saying. He's not a real rabbi, anyway, just the manager of the cemetery, but he says some nice prayers and he gives us each a handful of dirt to throw on the casket. Midge and Milt Pippick are there with their kids, Max and Alice, and the Zingers from next door, with a smattering of other longtime neighbors and the ladies from bingo, who tug at their polyester dresses in the heat. There's a party after at the bingo club, but I don't want to go. I ride my bike home from the service once it's over.

My last day with her replays in my mind. The lock on the bathroom door is broken and she turned the knob while I was on the toilet and I shouted, "Don't come in here!" Those were my last words to my mother.

I miss work for a few days. Wally Nortweller pings me. "Take as much time as you need," he says. "The Panther protocol meeting is on Friday at three."

At night I eat ramen noodles for dinner. I set up the Scrabble board and play both of our racks. I don't play the high tiles when it's my turn, and when it's her turn I get up and move into her chair. I lean back and look at the tiles from far away. I try to see things through her eyes. I look at my empty seat and imagine that I'm her, looking at me.

Then I know I'm getting maudlin so I start drinking beer and not cleaning up my dishes or putting my clothes away. I lie in bed at night and think that I might turn her bedroom into a TV room. I always wanted a flat screen TV. It would be like a home theater. I get up and turn on the computer and type "Flat Screen TVs" into the search box. An endless stream of pictures fills the monitor. I click through them one by one and scratch at the bug bite on top of my shoulder.

I wonder if a forty-two-inch screen is too big. I look at the pictures and try to imagine it. I feel a sharp prick from the bump on my shoulder, as if I have cut it with my fingernail. I dab it gently. It's swelling now, the size of a wadded up piece of chewing gum. It feels like a spider bite.

I go into the bathroom and turn on the light. I pull up my shirt and look at my shoulder in the mirror. It's splotchy and raised like a gumdrop. It pulses with blood under the surface. I pull my shirt off to get a closer look, but I can't make out the edges or what the dark streaks are made of. It's wrinkled and puckered. *What are the odds*, I think. *I get a cancerous mole the same week my mother dies.*

I open the bathroom drawer and hold up her magnifying mirror. I blink hard when I see it. *I am that person who sees Jesus in a piece of toast.* I hold up the mirror again and have another look. I don't know how much beer I've been drinking, but coiled snugly on my shoulder just above my right scapula: a blob, a bulb, a staring little acorn. It's my mother.

I know it's just the grief. I open the medicine cabinet and take three sleeping pills and wash them down with beer. I crawl back into bed and close my eyes. Before I can count to three, I'm in a cold and dreamless slumber.

In the morning the mole is still there, an ashy lump, and there's no denying it. It has my mother's soft cheeks, her curled fingers. She wears a simple housedress and brown loafers, her sensible shoes. Her eyes are closed in peaceful rest. I put on a shirt, a sweater and a jacket and ride my bike to the office. Enough of this wallowing.

Shake it off. The air is crisp and the city sparkles with morning dew. Shake it off, man. Shake it off.

"Since when do you sweat like this?" My mother's voice pierces my reverie. I hit a pothole and nearly bounce us both onto the pavement.

"This is an auditory hallucination," I say out loud.

"Oh, big words," my mother says. "I'm drowning back here. Your father never sweat like this. I never sweat like this."

"Please," I beg, though I don't know to whom.

"You don't get this from me," Mother sniffles. Either she heeds my plea or the sweat makes her uncomfortable. She sulks in silence the rest of the way.

At work, she rides shotgun on my shoulder, peeking at my computer screen as I type a message to Wally. She offers tidbits of advice and admonitions. "That doesn't make any sense," she frets. "That's not even English."

"It's a draft," I whisper. "It's not supposed to make sense."

"Why do it twice when you can do it right once?" she says. "Say, 'Each person has the authority to bend the rules to help the customer.' Why say 'empower'? Since when is empower a verb?"

"Mother, please!"

My shoulder slackens and then it goes cool. I have hurt her feelings. My ears ring with the quiet.

"I see what you mean, though," I soften. "It's better the way you said it. How did you put it again?"

My shoulder warms up. "Each person can... how did I put it? Now I've lost it." I can hear the excitement in her voice. She chatters quietly in my ear all morning and I do whatever she says. I need to buy some time.

In the afternoon, I hear the lilting rattle of her snore. I take the chance to go to the bathroom with a little privacy. I've been holding it for hours. The relief is overwhelming. When I'm done, I sit on the toilet and try to make a plan. This is her dream come true, I realize. She's with me all the time. She has a real job in an office, and finally we can be the team she always wanted. She'll never leave me, I think, and I feel guilty for thinking it as soon as I do. I should be elated. I have my mother back.

I put my sweater over my shoulders and head to the Panthers meeting at three. Wally is telling a joke to the group when I walk in and sit down next to Hannah. I catch the tail end of it, something about a soufflé and an oven, and everyone roars with laughter. When Wally was our teammate, no one laughed at his stupid jokes. Now that he's the manager, it's like he's Dana Carvey. Drafts of motivational posters from our animal collection are pinned on the wall. One has two alligators creeping out of a moat grinning while a man's leg walks out of the frame. The word "Teamwork" is below in ornate cursive. Another poster shows a winking camel with the words "Find Beauty."

Wally gets down to business. "I come to you with an open kimono," Wally says. "I want us all to sing from the same sheet of music today. I want us to walk out of here knowing that we've picked the low-hanging fruit. I want Christmas lights, people. There's no reason why we can't be cooking with gas for the whole quarter."

"I don't get that," my mother whines, muffled under wool. I tighten the sweater around my neck and look straight ahead. I spend the rest of the meeting with my hand resting lightly on my shoulder.

The hours stretch on while my mother goes through cycles of sleep and wakefulness. When she's on, she's on. She tells me what to buy on the way home to cook for dinner. She wants me to have a barbecue this weekend and invite the ladies from the bingo club. "You and I should take a cruise together!" Mother says. "I always wanted to sail the Pacific Ocean."

She tells me if I focus I can get promoted and move to a cubicle by a window. I glance around to see if anyone can hear us. "Look, Mom," I say. "I appreciate your input, but can you dial it back a little? I've got a handle on things myself."

She moistens. I can tell she's tearful. "I just want what's best for you, honey," she says.

"I want..."

I can't finish my thought because Hannah peeks her head around the corner of my cubicle.

"Hey stranger," she says.

I pull the sweater up around my neck.

"Hey."

"How are you feeling these days?" She slides down the wall and sits cross-legged on the floor.

"I'm doing fine," I answer.

"I'm glad to see you back here. I was getting worried about you. I'm real sorry about your mom."

"Who is this?" Mother whispers.

"No," I say reflexively.

"No what?" Hannah asks.

"No... no..." I flounder. "You shouldn't worry about me. I'm doing fine."

"I was thinking," Hannah says. She twirls a charm on her brace-let with her finger. "I'd like to take you out to dinner some time. To cheer you up."

"Oh," I say. Blood rushes to my cheeks, and other places. "That would be awesome."

"I don't like this girl," my mother chides. "Look at those fingernails." I look at Hannah's slender graceful hands. "Each nail is a different length. That's just grooming."

"Well, good," Hannah says, standing up. "Any night this week. Or next week. You pick it."

"I will," I say.

"Okey doke," she says. Her footsteps shoosh down the hallway.

"Tidy fingernails say a lot about a person, Owen," Mother says. "It's such a simple thing to do."

"Hush," I whisper.

Hannah and I pick Saturday night and she suggests Giuseppe's Pizzeria. It's a real Italian place with tablecloths and everything, despite the way it sounds. I shower and dry off and Mom and I chat while I comb my wet hair in the bathroom. I lean in to splash on some new cologne.

"Don't put on aftershave," she tells me. "Women don't like aftershave. It was a man who invented aftershave. No woman likes it."

"It's not aftershave," I say. "It's cologne."

"Your father just naturally smelled good. He smelled like pine nuts. He smelled good no matter what."

I put down the bottle and look at her in the mirror. "Can you see him?" I ask her.

"What are you talking about?" she says.

"I mean…" I say. I shake my head. "I don't mean anything. Forget it. I'm just nervous about tonight."

"Don't be nervous, Owen," she says warmly. "You deserve to have

a good time tonight and this girl is lucky to go out with you. Just
relax and have fun."

"Thanks, Mom," I say. "That means a lot to me." I open the bathroom drawer and take out a Band-Aid. I bend my shoulder toward
the light in the reflection.

"What are you doing?" she asks.

"I... I figured..." I should have brought this up sooner. "I thought
I'd have some privacy tonight."

"You can't be serious," Mom says. "Owen. Think about what this
means to me. To be able to go to an Italian restaurant. To be out in
the evening air. I can't believe..." She struggles to find the words.

I take the bandage and stuff it into my pocket. "I'm sorry, Mom.
I wasn't thinking. It'll be fun if we all go out. Really. I just was
a little nervous. Let's go get ready."

My shoulder softens and warms up. "Will you do something
for me, honey?"

"Sure," I say. "What is it?"

"Will you order the spaghetti and meatballs?"

At dinner the waitress takes our order and Hannah asks if
I want to split a Caesar salad.

"Do you really want all that garlic?" Mom whispers.

"That sounds great," I say. "And I'll have the spaghetti and
meatballs."

"I'll have the eggplant parmagiana," says Hannah. We hand our
menus to the waitress.

Mom's annotations funnel to my ear. "You know they buy that
house wine by the jug and just quadruple the price of it. You have
no idea what you're getting when you have the house wine."

"You know what I heard?" says Hannah, leaning in.

"I didn't hear anything," I say. I take a sip of my wine.

"I heard that we're having another re-org and a relo. Wally got a job at PulPerfection. We're getting migrated into Training and Development."

"Oh, Owen!" Mother titters.

"You should apply for Wally's job," I tell Hannah.

"What?" says Mother. "*You* apply, Owen. Why are you planting this idea in her head?"

"That's sweet of you to say," says Hannah. She swirls her wine around. "I don't have as much experience. But I was thinking I might ask about it."

"You totally should," I say.

"I don't understand you," says my mother. Her breath is warm. "It's like you *want* to fail. Why do you do this?"

I know the food is about to come, but I excuse myself and go into the bathroom. I check the stalls once I'm in there, and then I can barely keep my temper.

"I'm on a *date*, Mom! You have to give me some space. You have to be quiet!"

She sighs. "Owen, you misunderstand me. You always have. You're making tonight about me."

"That's just my point," I pout. I pace the bathroom floor.

"I'm not what's holding you back, Owen."

"Look," I say. "Can we just agree to do it my way tonight? Can you please just sit quietly and let me talk to her and make my own decisions? Right or wrong?"

"I won't say a word."

"Thank you," I say. I wash my hands as if to prove I had a reason to go to the bathroom, and head toward the door.

"By the way," she giggles, "can you get over how many times she says the word 'like'? 'I'll, like, have the eggplant. I, like, want that job.' She doesn't even hear herself."

My fist tightens around the Band-Aid in my pocket. I take it out and before she can speak I cover her and press down the tape. "I'm sorry, Mom," I say. "It's just for an hour. Just... chill for..." I trail off. My shoulder twitches. Then it's quiet. I open the door and walk back to the table.

The food is there, and Hannah has waited for me to start.

"Sorry," I say, tucking my napkin into my lap. "This looks fantastic."

Hannah points to a dapper man with a curled moustache and handkerchief in his coat pocket seated at the next table, who I think must be Giuseppe. "Get a load of that guy's aftershave," she whispers. "I can smell it all the way from here."

We drove separate cars to the restaurant so I walk Hannah to hers after dinner. The air is warm and it's still light out, even though it's late. She stands against her car door. "That was fun," she says. "Thanks." Before I can say anything, she puts her hand on my shoulder and leans in and kisses me. The spot on my shoulder is sore beneath her touch.

"Ow," I say.

"What's wrong?"

"It's nothing. It's just a funny mole. It's a little tender, is all."

Her face turns serious. "A funny mole is a big deal, Owen. My uncle had a sore mole and it turned out to be cancer. You have to get that looked at."

"I'll get it looked at," I say. I wish I could go back to when she was kissing me.

"I'm not kidding. My uncle nearly died. A mole shouldn't hurt."

"I promise I'll get it looked at," I say.

"I'll see you on Monday," says Hannah.

I knock on her roof three times once she gets in and starts her car, and wave as she drives away.

Once I'm home, I slip off my coat and clear my throat. "I'm taking it off now," I say.

I unbutton my shirt. With a quick tug, I pull off the tape. She's withdrawn, shadowed. She's more shrunken than before.

"Mom?" I say. "Are you okay?"

Nothing moves.

"Mom?"

My heart races until I notice her little chest rising and falling. "I know you're in there, Mom," I say. "I can see you breathing."

"Don't speak to me," she says without opening her eyes.

"Can we just talk about this? Like adults?" I ask. "There has to be some compromise."

"Smothering me under a pillow is not a compromise, Owen."

"It wasn't like that," I soothe. "You went on dates without me before I was born. I should get to go on dates now, too."

"Your body, your choice," she says unhappily. She opens her eyes and blinks. "What time is it?"

I check my watch. "9:30."

"Oh, turn on the TV. I want to watch Judge Judy."

I grab a beer, lie on the sofa, and click the remote. Sure enough, Judge Judy is there, eying a cocky-looking teenager in a shirt and tie. "Maybe you stopped at the stop sign," she tells him. "And maybe I'll come down there and dance a polka."

"Yes, ma'am," he says respectfully, but he can't stop grinning.

I pop open the beer and we settle in for the evening.

I am walking on the moon. My feet glide beneath me, pumping in time to Michael Jackson's "Bad" pulsing through the earphones. I dance, groove, get down on the sidewalk outside a busy public market while a small crowd forms around me, but I dance for an audience of one. Hannah watches, laughing. *Yeah.* I pivot off a bike rack, spin. Hannah says something but I can only see her sweet lips move. I pull one earphone from my ear. "There's a drip," she says. I wait for her to say more. "Can you hear it? There's a drip."

"What?" I say.

Her voice gets coarser around the edges. "There's a drip."

The room is dark. My head feels thick from drinking and my neck is stiff. I watch the talking heads on the late night news. My shoulder prickles. Mother is awake. "A drip, Owen," she says. "It's driving me crazy."

I hold the stillness, feel the dampness of the beer can.

She waits for a moment. "Am I talking to myself here?"

"I don't hear it," I say.

"Well, I'm a lot of things," she says, "but crazy isn't one of them. And last time I checked, I wasn't deaf."

I rub my thumb along the can.

"How can you not hear it?" she says. "I can't hear myself think. Do something, Owen. I'd do it myself, but I can't. I wouldn't ask if I weren't in this position."

"I don't hear it," I say again. My teeth grind in my mouth.

She waits.

"Owen, it's driving me crazy. Are you going to do something about it, or not?"

"Okay," I tell her. I get up and stumble toward the hallway. I'm still thick-headed from my dream, but a tingling settles over me.

Mother is right. She's not what's holding me back.

"It's not over here. Can't you hear it? Owen, what's the matter with you?"

I drop the beer on the carpet and it spills out in a marshy puddle. "Owen! Are you drunk? Get the seltzer and a rag."

The room is spinning. "I need to ask you a favor, Mom," I say. "What is it, honey?"

I go into the kitchen and grab a tray of ice cubes. "It's a big favor."

I take the tray and walk into the study. "Tell me what you need, Owen," she says. "What are you looking for in here?" I find what I want and head into the bathroom.

I turn on the light and look into the mirror. I feel the quick intake of her breath. "Our situation has nothing to do with Hannah's uncle," she says. "You're mixing apples and oranges here."

I twist the ice tray and lift a cube into my hand. I raise the ice to my shoulder and hover over her. "It's not about her uncle, Mom. It's not even about her," I say. "I just feel…"

My shoulder pulsates. She squeezes into a tight little knot.

I can't do it. I lower the cube to the sink. Then I slide down to the linoleum floor.

"I don't know how to handle this," I say.

"You're handling it fine, Owen. Don't overthink things. You always overthink things."

My arms fall to my sides and my eyelids feel heavy. "Maybe I am."

"You are. You're just like your father." She chuckles. "I loved the man, but he couldn't choose which pants to wear without my help. Do you remember what he was like?"

All at once, I do.

A wave of nausea climbs in my throat.

"Forgive me," I say.

Her voice echoes back to me, distant and tinny. I stand up and rub the ice over her until water drips down my chest. Then I take the X-Acto knife and hold it between my thumb and forefinger, and with my other hand, I pinch and pull her away from my skin. She doesn't fight me. Slowly, I drag the blade in a circle around her. I saw back and forth. She is softer than I expected.

When I finish with the cutting, she pops out like a little ball. Sticky strands trail in her wake. I hold her in my hand.

"Mom?" I whisper. "Can you hear me?"

She's curled up in the fetal position, her hands tucked underneath her chin. She is folded in prayer.

"Mom?" I say louder. "Mom?"

I'm stunned. I stroke her lightly but she's cold and gummy and she sticks to my forefinger. I wipe her back onto my palm.

I hold her for a while and then I don't know what to do with her. I can't keep her on the mantle. I don't want to bury her. Finally, I lift the lid to the toilet seat and carefully drop her in the water.

"Goodbye, Mommy," I say. "I love you. I love you. I love you."

She circles the bowl a few times, and then she's gone.

SLEEPING GIANTS IN THE DAYLIGHT

Elaine Panopolis was woefully inadequate. This was documented fact. In college, a professor had written it in red capital letters across the top of her final paper: *WOEFULLY INADEQUATE.* In the coloring of years it had amplified and now Elaine took it to apply to her whole life. In fact, the professor had written, "Your footnotes are woefully inadequate" in simple black ink at the end, but what did that matter now?

She would like to say she used to be strong and had only been thrown off-kilter recently, but that would not be true. Elaine had never been strong. She had never felt indestructible, never stood atop a sand dune and shouted down the waves. She never loved Andrew Bang; she never even liked him. Their first kiss, on a street corner after three rounds of beers: the cool night breeze, on her tiptoes in his arms. Elaine thought, "This is what it feels like to kiss a rubber mannequin." She had been taking CPR classes, touching her lips to the Resusci Annie doll, pressing down against the dead girl's mouth and giving her a second chance at life, only to watch her die again. That was what kissing Andrew had felt like. Like pressing against death, staving it off for a while. Andrew had laughed, then belched, and death wafted over her. She knew then that Andrew had her: that he was the only one who would ever want her; that she would never have the strength to leave.

Andrew spared her the pain of having to face that test, though, because after four fraught years of dating, Andrew finally left her.

Now Elaine rented a room eight blocks from her old place on California Street, sharing a house with a middle-aged painter named Dorothy who made giant canvasses with deep splotches of color that hung in every room. The whole place reeked of cat urine, or somehow just of cat, even though there was only one cat in the house, one sole survivor left after four became three and then two and then one. The cat, named Shrapnel, was a bony twenty-year-old tortoiseshell, and every time Elaine stroked its skull she felt as if she was telling it her last quiet goodbyes.

Dorothy, who went by Doro, was tall and didn't have an inside voice and had red hair she kept off her face with colorful scarves. She had inherited the house from her grandmother and, with no mortgage to pay, supported herself by taking in roommates and occasionally selling a painting. Her second week there, Elaine had found a man sitting at the kitchen table who looked embarrassed when she pulled open the sliding glass door and discovered him eating a grilled cheese sandwich. Doro was scrubbing the sink with a Brillo pad and talking to the man with her back to Elaine. "It's the cost of doing business. The price we pay. No one wants to live in a Communist country," Doro said, elbows jabbing outward as she scrubbed the porcelain. The man was pale and lanky, with curly auburn chest hairs peeking out of a crumply denim shirt. He smiled at Elaine apologetically and she slipped past him and into her room. It turned out this was Doro's married boyfriend, Franz, who came by some afternoons, and Elaine would hear Doro scream and weep at him sometimes in her bedroom with the door closed.

Now three months in, Doro was sitting under the hot July sun in their yard the day after one of these tearful arguments when Elaine opened the back door to let out the cat. Franz had gone home, Elaine imagined, wherever that might be. Doro held a glass of iced tea in her hand and stared ahead at the chain link fence that demarcated their patch of asphalt and spotty grass. A plate with crumbs from her breakfast sat on the ground beside her. Shrapnel picked his way through the weeds and sniffed at dandelions, first making his way toward Doro and then, changing his mind, curling up where he was.

Elaine found herself walking toward Doro as well. She stood for a moment behind her, feeling a flash of panic at having wandered this far into the yard without a reason and finding it too late to turn back. Doro looked up.

"Fucking sunshine," she said. Her fair skin shone with sweat. "I'm too Irish for this shit."

"Want me to get you a hat?" Elaine offered.

Doro faced forward again. "You're sweet." She said it with a flatness that confused Elaine. She didn't know if it was a description or an acceptance of the offer.

"Pull up a chair," Doro said.

Elaine walked to the paved area under the deck and dragged out a low folding chair with a canvas seat. She plopped down in it next to Doro, the tall grass scratching the undersides of her knees.

"Got any big plans for the weekend?" asked Doro. She sipped her iced tea.

"I haven't thought about it yet." It was nearly one o'clock on a Saturday. "I have laundry. I should probably give my mom a call."

"You're a good daughter. I should have known," said Doro. "We could go to the beach. Want to go to the beach?"

Elaine had never socialized with Doro before. Elaine had not socialized with anyone, in fact, for months. She hadn't even realized she didn't have friends anymore until Andrew ended it and she didn't know whom to call. She would make new friends when she was ready. Perhaps she would be friends with Doro.

"That sounds fun," Elaine said, in a tone that seemed appropriate for the occasion.

"Yeah?" said Doro. She turned and looked more animated. "Yeah, let's do it. Cool. Let's get our suits on."

Doro stood up and walked toward the house. Shrapnel stayed curled in the grass but followed her with his gaze. Doro paused at the door. "Can you drive?" she said. "My car needs oil."

Elaine's car needed gas. But yes. The beach with Doro. Yes. Elaine would drive.

She rooted around in her dresser and couldn't find her bathing suit. She'd packed up sloppily and shoved things haphazardly in the new place. All the drawers were emptied out onto the bed when Doro poked her head in, wearing a turquoise 1950s-style one-piece with thick straps over her shoulders and a floppy bow between her breasts. She wore large starlet sunglasses and a straw hat and had put on bright red lipstick. A sarong was tied around her waist. Elaine felt caught when she saw her, as if she had been rifling through Doro's dresser instead of her own.

"You moving out?" said Doro, surveying the clothes spilled everywhere.

"I'm just looking for my bathing suit," said Elaine. Strangely, she was trembling. She picked up a sweatshirt to distract from her shaky hands. "I know I have one. I just don't know where I put it."

"Borrow mine," said Doro. "It's a two piece. It'd fit you. It has a bandeau top."

She was gone before Elaine could answer. Doro came back with a red bikini with beaded tassels hanging off it and at just that moment Elaine spotted her black one-piece mixed in with her bras and underwear. She grabbed it and held it up. "I found it! No worries!"

Doro shrugged and walked down the hallway. Elaine squeezed into the bathing suit, remembering how unflattering it had been even when it was new, and now the elastic was shot and it offered no support anywhere. It actually cupped into a little gap right at the crotch when she sat down, but she didn't have it in her to wear Doro's bikini. She pulled shorts on and flip-flops and rubbed sticky sunscreen onto her face. Her stomach growled and she wished she'd eaten breakfast.

She presented herself to Doro in the living room. "I'm ready!"

Doro looked her up and down and smiled. "Cool beans," she said. "*Allons-y.*"

They turned on Fulton and went down the Avenues. Sometimes the fog rolled in the higher the numbers went, but not today. Doro sat comfortably slumped with her legs crossed wide and her foot resting on the glove compartment. Around 38th Avenue, she sat up straight and looked around.

"Slow down," she said.

"Why?" asked Elaine, letting her foot off the gas.

"Slow down. Pull over. On the corner."

Elaine turned on her signal and saw Franz at the same time. He was there, smiling, lifting his hand in an awkward half-wave. He wore long shorts and another of his crumpled button-down shirts, a green windbreaker, flip-flops, and some kind of fishing hat. He carried a large canvas bag. Elaine pulled up alongside him.

"Ladies!" he said, sliding into the back seat. He reached forward and patted Doro on the shoulder. "You're going to get burned today, dear."

"I better not," she said warningly.

"Hi, Elaine," he said pleasantly.

"Hi, Franz." She didn't know where he had come from or how long he had been standing there, but she had an idea why she hadn't picked him up at his house. No one spoke for several blocks.

Doro broke the silence. She drew her words out long and hard. "How's *Shir*-ley?"

"Shirley's getting by," he answered. There was a quiet chastising in his tone.

Elaine saw the peaks of the windmill by the beach up ahead.

"Franz is afraid to leave his wife," Doro said, turning her head to Elaine and explaining, as if complicitly.

"I have left my wife, Doro. Be fair."

"Franz is afraid to leave his wife because she can't live by herself, because she doesn't know how, because she's very frail and needs him very much," said Doro.

Elaine made a smile. "I see."

"Doro likes to exaggerate," Franz said warmly, giving her shoulder another squeeze.

"Doro doesn't like to get dicked around," Doro answered.

"Okay," Franz acquiesced, leaning back.

"I see water!" said Elaine, and she crossed the Great Highway and pulled into the parking lot.

They picked their way over a reedy dune and plodded down the sand. Clusters of people dotted the beach walking dogs, sitting in low folding chairs, or standing over children who squatted at the water's edge. A couple of elderly women stood at the shoreline looking out and talking to each other, and a trio of gangly teenage boys played hacky sack. Doro spread a thin cotton blanket and the three of them sat down and began peeling off shoes and shirts.

"Come," said Franz kindly to Doro, who shuffled over to him. He rubbed white sunscreen onto her back and shoulders. When he finished, he turned to Elaine. "You too," he said.

Elaine glanced at Doro but she was eating a banana and looking at the horizon.

"Come on," Franz repeated. He already had lotion squirted in his palm.

Elaine walked over, sat with her back to him and lowered her head. "Thanks," she said. Franz spread lotion generously onto her back. He rubbed it on the sides of her neck and down her arms. He ran his warm palms across her back to the curves of her waist, where his fingertips met the edges of her swimsuit. Elaine kept her head down until he was done. "You're good," he said, giving her shoulder a squeeze. "Can you do me?"

He shifted his back to her. Elaine looked to Doro. Doro bit into her banana and raised her eyebrows at Elaine. "Have at it," she said.

Elaine squirted sunscreen onto her palms and moved her hands along Franz's back. It was rough with acne scars and dotted with moles. It was strong and muscular.

"Okay," she said when she finished. "Did you bring anything to eat?"

"Have anything you like," he answered.

She reached into his bag. Two small, homegrown-looking apples. A container of Nutella.

"Are there any more bananas?" she asked.

"Sorry," said Doro. "Last one."

Elaine's stomach tingled with hunger.

It was a lovely day for the beach. The waves sparkled and frothed and changed color with the currents from green to blue to deep black. Further down the shoreline, big black rocks sat like sleeping giants in the daylight. Nearby signs warned of rip currents and dangerous surf. It wasn't much of a swimming beach and the water was numbingly cold, but Elaine could see windsurfers in wetsuits riding crests in the distance and men with their pants cuffs rolled up standing knee-deep in the water. She lay facedown on the blanket. Franz was talking about a "Re-Birthing a New You" life coaching conference he had just come back from: five days of sitting cross-legged and crafting personal mission statements and learning to be your best self. Doro had gone through the program two years before and had been trying to get Elaine to go as well. It cost four thousand dollars.

Franz was describing an exercise from the workshop that involved sitting in a circle with a dozen people who had just been pretend-shipwrecked. They crowded on an imaginary life raft that accommodated ten people and had to convince the group why they should be allowed to stay on board. At the end, the group took a vote and two people were pretend-thrown to sea.

"I said I am a patient man and I see all sides of a problem. This is a valuable skill because one needs patience and perspective in threatening times," said Franz.

"How is that empowering?" Elaine asked. "Choosing which people die, that sounds terrible to me."

"No, dear," said Franz, "you're looking at it the wrong way. Of course every creature deserves to live. What would you say if you *had* to, though? You must know the answer to this question. It's transformative to articulate your value."

"I don't know," said Elaine. She twirled a fraying strand on the blanket. "I don't think so. Everybody has the same right to live. No human being has less value than another."

"That's ridiculous," said Doro, sitting on the other side of her. "A rapist should live just as much as you should? What if it was you and Hitler? Would you jump off the raft so Hitler could survive?"

"Okay, no," said Elaine. "Not if the person were going to kill thousands of people or rape them. Or kill one person. Without a good reason."

"So you're saying you would do it if it would save another person's life, but not your own, then," said Franz. "You're still not answering the question."

"I recognize I have value," said Elaine. "I'm not saying I don't. I'm just saying..."

She didn't want to explain this. She didn't *need* to be the kind of person who would throw someone overboard. She didn't want to judge Doro and Franz but she was appalled that this choice came so easily to them.

"You should do the program," Franz said. "I think you'd find it enlightening."

Doro let out a snort.

It was too soon for Elaine to make new friends, she realized. She didn't have her footing.

Elaine closed her eyes and let the sounds of the beach wash over her. Doro and Franz continued talking in quiet tones and the cries of the boys playing hacky sack mingled with the calls of gulls overhead. Elaine squeezed sand in her hands and let the sun warm her. She wondered how late in the afternoon it was and what time it had been when they left. She still had to do her laundry.

Franz rummaged in his canvas bag. "You're getting pink," he said – to Doro, Elaine assumed. But then his hands were on her, smoothing hot lotion up her calves and thighs. She turned in surprise.

"I'm okay," she said.

Franz left his hand on her calf. "Don't be foolish, Elaine."

Elaine wasn't sure what to do.

"Yes, don't be foolish, Elaine," Doro echoed.

Elaine twisted to look at Doro, who stared at her from behind big sunglasses. "I'm not worried about it, if that's what you're thinking," Doro said. "Franz knows if he ever cheated on me I'd cut off his balls."

Elaine turned back to Franz. "I'm okay. Thanks, though." She rested her face back down on her arms and shut her eyes. *God, these two.*

Franz didn't answer. He ran his hands up and down Elaine's legs anyway, along the back of her thighs, all the way to the bottom of her bathing suit. He pressed along the edge of the seam. He traced his fingertips back and forth along her thigh.

Doro didn't say a word. She stood up and walked into the ocean.

Elaine felt Doro's absence in the air around her, but her mind had gone to static. It had been so long since any man had touched her, she had forgotten what it felt like. It was bad, and it was soft, and it was good, and she didn't want him to stop. Something inside her had gone into override.

Franz massaged Elaine's legs. He pressed his knuckles into the soles of her feet and tugged at each of her toes. He leaned forward and pressed into her shoulders and she felt the huff of his breath behind her, sensed the heft of his weight above her. He stretched her neck long. He slid his hand under her suit at her crotch and at the same time that Elaine opened her eyes, he pressed his finger deep between her legs.

"Hey!" she said. She torqued herself up but he blocked her in the sand. "Get off me!" she barked, and pushed her hand against his chest.

He released her. She scuttled across the blanket. Franz still smiled at her warmly, as if she was sweet and a bit silly and had just been shown a scary spider.

"We'll teach you some lessons this summer, dear," he said. "By the end of August you'll not remember the girl you once were."

"What the fuck are you talking about?" Elaine scrabbled around the blanket, gathering her clothes and belongings.

Franz looked disappointed. "I'm sorry if I upset you," he pouted. "You never said no to anything. You can't say that you ever told me no."

Elaine's hands shook as she shoved aside towels and banana peels searching for her car keys. She stood up and saw Doro standing knee-deep in the water, her back to the horizon, staring up at them. Doro held her hand over her eyes, shading them from the sun. Elaine stared back. Out of nowhere, a sneaker wave rose up behind Doro and slowly pushed her off her feet. She stumbled and fell facedown. Then Doro was gone.

Everything else was the same. The wave lapped the shore and recessed, smoothing back onto the ocean's surface. Elaine gaped at the spot where Doro had been standing. She squinted and waited and tried to make sense of... just, anything.

"Did you see that?" she asked Franz.

"See what?" he answered. He sat on the blanket looking up at her.

"Doro. She fell into the water. You didn't see that?"

Franz looked at the sea.

"I don't see her. Where are you looking?"

Nothing. Then all at once Doro's hands jutted out of the water an impossible distance from where she had fallen in.

"There! There!" Elaine shouted.

"Doro!" Franz called out. He stood up and ran to the water's edge. Elaine followed in a numb half-jog. "Doro!" he called again.

He turned to Elaine. "I can't swim," he said, stricken. "I can't swim."

Franz stood there like a jackass, arms hanging uselessly at his sides.

Then he roared. "*I can't swim!*"

Elaine found her legs splashing into the water, clumsy as logs. Her arms flailed and the shallow sea floor went on forever. Finally, she flung herself belly-first into the waves and swam out toward Doro. The water was freezing. She knew it would be, yet it stunned her anyway. Salt water blurred her eyes and flowed into her nose and mouth. Her chest felt thin, her heart huge and pounding. She heaved for air in shallow gasps as she slapped forward in the water. The current was in her favor.

Doro's face was contorted with horror when Elaine finally reached her. Her hair was soaked and her sunglasses were gone. Her eyes were wild with fear and she gulped for air in a panic. She grabbed Elaine's arm and pulled her down. They both submerged. Elaine yanked free and Doro grabbed her again.

"No!" yelled Elaine. Doro fought the ocean desperately. She grasped Elaine's shoulder and again pulled her under. Cold water rushed up Elaine's nose as they grappled. Doro's hands clawed at her and salt water choked her throat. Finally, Elaine broke the surface. "Get off me!" she screamed, and with her palm she pushed Doro's head underwater. She held it there until Doro let her go.

Elaine wrapped her arm around Doro's chest and side-kicked back toward shore, gulping and gasping as they went. Doro rode stiffly on top of Elaine at first, for what seemed like minutes, and then she went limp. "Doro?" said Elaine.

Elaine's heel hit the sand. The teenage boys were suddenly there and they lifted Doro by the arms and another man ran into the surf and helped them carry her in. Elaine stumbled behind them and collapsed on the beach.

The boys lay Doro on her back and Franz leaned over her, shaking her by the shoulders.

"Turn her on her side," Elaine said. She dragged herself over and checked Doro's pulse, then rolled her over. Water spilled out of her mouth. She laid her flat again, lifted her neck, closed her nostrils and breathed steadily against Doro's lips. One, two, three. One, two, three. One, two, three. One, two, three. Doro coughed and spit water into Elaine's mouth, then began to cry. Franz moved in and knelt beside her. "My darling," he said.

"Elaine!" Doro wailed. "Elaine!"

"I'm here," Elaine answered. She clasped Doro's hands in hers.

"You saved me," Doro wept. "You saved me." She gazed up pathetically. "The wave knocked me over. It was so cold I couldn't catch my breath."

"You're all right now," Elaine told her. Doro cried while the onlookers stared.

Doro moaned and sobbed and when her cries slowed down Elaine extricated herself. She let Franz take her place. Wet sand matted his hair and stuck to his pasty legs. Doro curled into him, the two of them locked in a burled knot of dysfunction.

"Okay," Elaine said to no one. Her skin was cold and tacky from the salt, and her body vibrated. It occurred to her that everyone had been wrong about her, about every single thing, for her entire life. To a person, they could all go fuck themselves. She mapped out the distance from where she was standing to her keys, from her keys to the car, from the car to the Great Highway.

Elaine began to walk.

TOREADOR

You say you want to be like Hemingway.

"In what way?" I ask.

"In every way," you answer. "The life is the writing. The writing is life. There is no space between man and creation. Creation and God." We're on our first date in a hotel bar – bright lights and worn maroon carpet – waiting for a hot fudge sundae. On a TV set in the corner, Walter Cronkite says Skylab has pierced the atmosphere, a burning trail of fire.

"Didn't Hemingway shoot himself in the chest?" I ask.

You laugh at me. "You're looking at it from the wrong angle, Betty. Think of the running of the bulls, the roar of the crowd at a bullfight."

"Do you know that bulls are colorblind?" I say. "It's the motion of the cape that gets them. The cape hides the matador's sword. They use red to mask the blood."

The waitress brings our sundae, lays down two long spoons. Her earrings are thick white hoops and her hair smells like Breck shampoo. I scrape chocolate from the side and lick the spoon.

"You're not like anyone I've ever met before," you say, and I wonder if you know how many women men have said that to, Robert. You lean in and kiss me, once on the forehead and once on the cheek, and I'm startled by your gesture. An ambush, yet deferential. I think: *I should leave now. This can't go anywhere good.* But then we are dating, and then we are married, and I can't blame you for that.

Part Two

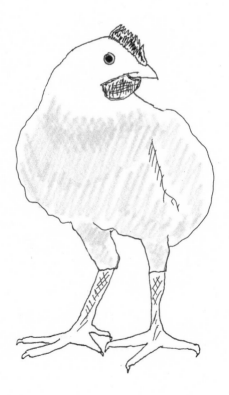

WHILE I AM AWAY

Dear Addison,

Thank you so much for dogsitting Niffy while I am at the "Re-Birthing a New You" Life Coaching conference. It's such a relief to me that you can come on short notice. What a coup that your dad is having bypass surgery so you're in town to visit from Chicago. It makes me a bit nervous to go away without meeting you face to face, but your craigslist ad in "Temporary Housing Sought" says you are an animal lover, and I have a good feeling about this.

Here are a few bits of information that will help you on your stay.

FOOD: Niffy gets two scoops of Dr. Phalangan's Organic Venison kibble every day at 5 p.m. She is also accustomed to eating the last bite of whatever you are having, and licking the plate when you are done. You don't have to do this, but if you don't do it, please give her extra affection at the end of the meal because she will probably be upset. You can stroke her head and along her muzzle and talk to her while you do this, and it should calm her down. If this doesn't work, you can open up a chamomile teabag and sprinkle it onto some warm rice with plain yogurt and a mushed up banana. This will relax her. Or you can just let her lick your plate.

STREET FOOD: She is not allowed to eat any "food" she finds on the street, and she knows this. She is allowed to dig in the yard next door and eat whatever "kitty almond roca" she finds buried by the neighbor's cat, Munch. The neighbor's name is Kimberly, and she has agreed to this. (San Encanto has a great mediation program, by the way, should you ever need it.)

WALKS: Niff-Niff gets two walks a day, one at 11 a.m. and one at 3 p.m. Hopefully you can coordinate your visits to your dad around this, as she will pee on her bedding if you are late. There are leash laws here so you have to put her on the long retractable leash when you go out (they do ticket), but make sure you let Niffy lead you and choose the route. She generally sticks to the sidewalk but there are a few "off-the-beaten" paths she likes to check out, so wear long pants to protect your legs from bramble. There's a cafe about six blocks north with a nice outdoor patio, and you can stop there and get a coffee. Technically you are not allowed to bring dogs onto the patio, so choose a table in the corner and do your best to keep Niff under your legs. This is especially crucial when you are letting her lick your plate.

GAMES: Her favorite game is when you get on the ground and pretend to be a dog with her. She does not like to play with the other dogs at the dog park (she is very smart and frankly is more interested in adult conversation) so it's important that she get the benefits of dog-like interactions from you. Basically, just get on your hands and knees in the living room, stick your butt in the air in a playful way, and wag it around a little while you growl at her and make occasional, sudden barks. She will watch you do this for a few minutes and then become engaged with you, doing the same movements back. Once she is interacting with you like this, you can swing your hips so that you knock into her with your butt, while barking. Also put your hand on top of her paw in a dominance gesture. She will "teethe" you and "mouth" you in an effort to reclaim dominance. This just means she is fully engaged and playing. She will not draw blood. If she does, just wipe it off and try not to get it on the carpet. It's important that you not chastise her for this, as it is normal canine behavior and would confuse her if you did, especially since you were the one who initiated it. If she hurts you and you can't conceal it from her and you have to stop playing, please placate and reassure her so she knows that it isn't her fault. She generally likes to play this game before bed, around 11 p.m. each night.

HYGIENE: Just a heads up: if you get your period while you are here, please use tampons and flush them down the toilet. If you use maxi-pads, don't toss them in the bathroom trash (or any trash can inside the house), as Niffster likes to shred them. Please wrap them in newspaper and bring them to the large garbage bin in the back yard and strap the lid down with a bungee cord. (The cord is important because she can get in the can without it and has been known to strew the shredded pads across the sidewalk... whoops!) If you can't figure out how to strap the cord back on in the criss-cross pattern after you take it off, have a look at Kimberly's can next door. She is a pro at it and apparently finds it something of a "big deal."

SPARE KEYS: If you get locked out, the nearest spare key is with my mother, Gert. She lives a half-hour away with my stepdad, Gebhardt, and it's fine if you call her in case of emergency. She has cataracts so she doesn't like to drive at night – but she will – so if you need anything at all, please don't hesitate to call her at any hour, day or night. If it rolls to her voicemail, keep calling and she does eventually pick up. If she sounds annoyed, just try to power through it. Don't take it personally. It's just the way she interacts with the world.

I tried to organize a key swap with my neighbors, but no one wanted to do it after the whole "maxi-pads-in-the-street" incident. Ironically, that was the incident that brought the neighborhood together, in my opinion – everyone came outside when they heard Kimberly screaming at me. Suddenly all the neighbors can communicate! "It's not appropriate that your dog shits on my property!" "My backyard is not a public thoroughfare!" Their arms all akimbo – everyone loves to egg on a fight. But I don't begrudge them their resistance. If it will bring people together, I am willing to take the fall for that.

If my mother doesn't pick up, you can also jimmy the bathroom window.

CONTACTS: You can reach me at any of the numbers below if you need me. By the way, I've left the conference brochure for you to look at. It's a really exceptional group. People who want to help others. People who are not afraid of connection. People who will not talk about setting boundaries with me, as if boundaries are a good thing, something to strive for, without realizing that boundaries are the precise thing that keeps people apart. They may have chapters in Chicago if you want to look into it when you get home. (Just as an aside, I have never been to the Windy City and you planted the seed in my head when you said you are from there. I've actually been looking into plane fares because I have some free time since I'm not technically working now. Maybe you could show me around – or I could stay at your place for a few days so we could be "even-steven." I don't want you to feel indebted to me for putting you up while your dad is recovering.) (You know, I am happy to go visit your dad if he is still in the ICU when I get back. I would like to do that for you.)

I think that's it, Addison. It means the world to me that you are going to take such good care of my Niff-Niff. I'm so very excited to do this, and so very hopeful. And while I am away, please reassure Niffy that I'm coming back for her, stronger and happier and with a support system in place, for both of us. I'm not leaving her. I don't want her to worry about that. Nothing bad will happen. There will be no grim consequences, as my therapist says. I have to step over this threshold now, and in one week I will come back. Please hold down the fort while I am gone, Addison. In the end, we only have each other.

With immense gratitude,

Spirit Rosenblatt

PARTY AT THE END OF THE WORLD

Betty Zinger sat in her favorite chair, an egg-shaped basket with a cushion seat that hung on a hook and chain from the living room ceiling. She looked out the large window at the canyon that cupped her home. Theirs was the last house on the cul-de-sac. She'd known she wanted to live here before she even saw the place. It was a gut thing. She was not one to go woo-woo with California vibes and auras, but with this house it had been undeniable.

She'd toured forty-nine houses – the one on Lemon Patch Lane had been number fifty. She'd carried a spiral notebook in her purse and logged the details of every one. Her husband, Robert, had given up after the first dozen (any one of which would have been fine, he said) and handed the search over to her. She relished the assignment. *Wrong, wrong, wrong.* Each house had been wrong, though none of them was awful. She'd loved strolling through them anyway, opening closet doors, imagining future lives.

When the agent told her about the house at the end of the cul-de-sac, Betty's stomach fluttered. This was it. She knew it. She went simply to confirm it. And there it was. *Right.* As if waiting for her all these years.

A single-story ranch-style, it crowned the tip of a gentle bulb of houses with garages and driveways and unassuming lawns. The neighbors were all friendly. Even the houses looked like they were friends, each one somehow speaking to the others in their muted likenesses. The houses backed onto a woodsy ravine that ringed their yards, too steep for the kids to play in and too wide for strangers to breach. It reminded her of a place called Echo Canyon, a serene spot in the middle of a lake that her grandfather used to take her to in his motorboat, where they'd quiet the engine and call out *"Hello!" "Where are you!" "I am here!"* and have their ghost selves call back to them the same.

There was no echo in the canyon on Lemon Patch Lane. No sound distortions or tricks of physics. Just a comforting vista that Betty liked to gaze at from her swinging egg chair, grateful to the house for having found her, for giving her a home.

Betty saw Robert's reflection in the window as he approached her from behind. Still handsome, lanky and sexy, he had the same soft, glossy hair he'd had the day she met him twenty-one years before. He'd had the same bounce to his step when he first approached her at a party, the same sheepish grin. He'd been fascinated with her, enamored, and Betty had eaten it right up. He was a journalist then, and he'd peppered her with questions that felt personal. He was curious, so interested in everything around him, including Betty, that she talked and talked and felt entirely set free. And he was beautiful, she could not forget that. She'd read that baby animals have giant eyes, eyes too big for their faces, so that adults want to protect them. Eyes so adorable it disarms predators. Robert's grin and hair and big brown eyes were like that. Evolutionary tricks that had disarmed Betty. Now? It was just the way he looked.

"I'm heading out," Robert said. He spoke to her reflection. "Just the crabs, right? Crabs and bread?"

"Crabs and bread. The crabs are under my name. They'll be waiting for you. Keep them in the cooler and come straight home, please."

"They're... I mean, they're dead, right?"

Betty swung the chair around and faced him. "Not yet, I'm afraid."

"Okay." He bent down and kissed her on the cheek, then headed toward the front door. "I might tell them it's their last night on earth on the way home. I might not tell them. I'm going to see how I feel."

Robert shrugged on his coat.

"Drive carefully," Betty said.

Robert closed the door behind him.

Betty and Robert were hosting the neighborhood New Year's Eve party. *Y2K.* 1999 would roll over into the new millennium and no one knew what would happen. They said computers would crash, planes would crash, the stock market would crash. The world as they knew it would end. Betty wasn't worried. They would eat crab and drink champagne and if the credit card machines stopped working, whoever made them would figure out how to fix them and then they would work again. Just to be safe, though, she'd had her daughter, Abby, fly back to UNH that morning. Why play chicken with uncertainties? Let them win sometimes and they tended to leave you alone.

Now the ivy groundcover in her backyard quivered. Betty scrunched her eyes and saw Nunkin, the wily dachshund who lived next door, wriggle out. He'd dug a hole under their fence from the Pippick's again. Nunkin saw Betty's face and lit up, his whole body wagging. He ran to the cracked-open sliding glass door and triumphantly paraded inside.

"Nunkin," Betty said. "This is not your home." She picked up the dog and dodged his wet tongue as his muzzle darted at her face. He was elated in her arms. She craned her neck up, to the side. "No, no," she said. "Stop kissing me, stop kissing me." But the dog slobbered and licked, leaving sticky residue. "For God's sake, Nunkin," Betty said. "Jesus Christ."

She held the dog like a baby and reached for a tea towel to wipe her cheeks. Then she pushed the sliding glass door open wider with her foot and walked with the dog to the backyard, searching for his hole this time. The sun warmed them and they both relaxed under its bright heat, Nunkin on a field trip in Betty's arms and Betty feeling suddenly productive.

There it was. Soft, brown dirt in a mound on either side of a small furrow that a rodent could have made. Betty kicked a rock into the gap and pressed it down with her sneaker. She kissed Nunkin on his soft forehead. "I love you, Nunky, but this is my house. Your house is over there." She gestured to Midge and Milt Pippick's place next door, the only two-story house on the circle. "You're fucking with my yard and you have to stop it." The dog licked Betty on the lips. She spat and tried to reach her mouth to her shoulder but could not.

Together they walked over to the neighbors'. Betty rang the bell. The Pippicks rarely locked their front door, but Betty still had her midwestern politeness. She waited.

Midge laughed when she saw Nunkin in Betty's arms. "Nunky," she said. "Where you been?" Midge wore an embroidered silk bathrobe over her blue jeans and tee shirt. She wore this, Betty knew, when she got ready to go out. She was the only person Betty had ever known who owned a vanity – an ornate furniture station whose sole purpose was to facilitate the application of makeup.

In her previous life, Betty would have walked right by someone like Midge, with her perfectly styled hair and matching sweater sets. Betty was more wash-and-wear, *New York Times* crossword puzzle. Midge kept a fully stocked candy drawer for her kids; Betty made her own spaghetti sauce because the store brands added sugar. But on Lemon Patch Lane they'd become fast friends. Like Betty, Midge had two children, Max and Alice. And like Betty, Midge stopped working when her kids were born – Midge leaving her job as a bank manager and Betty giving up her career in corporate communications. Being a stay-at-home mom stung Betty more than it did Midge, especially when Robert was travelling. It helped to have someone sharp and funny right next door to share the days. Their kids were in and out of each other's houses like they lived in one large compound. Once, when Betty ran out of eggs while she was cooking dinner, Midge stood on her balcony and tossed some down to her in her backyard below. To her amazement, not one of them broke.

As for Robert, he endured Midge's husband, Milt, a man he called "aggressively boring." But Milt was all right.

"You know tonight is nothing fancy," Betty said, nodding to the silk robe and routine it signaled.

"Come on, it's New Year's Eve," Midge said. "Maybe the last one we'll ever have."

"Tell me you don't believe that," said Betty. "Computers are like dishwashers. They're not gods."

"I'm still wearing my new dress. And you should dress up, too. When else are we going to?"

Nunkin squirmed in Betty's arms and she thrust him forward. "Here," she said. "He dug under the fence again."

Midge took the dog and kissed him on the nose. "Who's a bad boy?"

Over Midge's shoulder Betty saw her own son, Ollie, watching TV with Midge's son, Max. They both sat on the carpet.

"Ollie, honey," Betty called to him. "Shouldn't you and Max be practicing your show for tonight?"

Ollie turned and looked at her with scorn. "We're not doing a show at your party, Mom, I told you. It's not interesting."

"*Not interesting,*" Betty mouthed to Midge. "Sweetie, of course it's interesting," she said. "Everybody looks forward to your magic shows. It's the highlight of the party."

"Magic is not what you think it is, Mom. We've moved on."

There was a time – years – when Ollie and Max cared about nothing more than magic. They saved their allowances for weighted coins and coats with secret linings and put shows on in the driveway. All the little girls in the neighborhood had crushes on them. They went to magic camps and hung out with weird older men at magic conventions. (All the magicians at these conventions were men who seemed a bit greasy-haired and bereft, but Ollie and Max were enthralled by them: *professionals.*) Something changed when twelve became thirteen and then fourteen. What had seemed charming before became a social liability: Loser, Nerd, Freak. They'd aged out of the thing they loved the most. The boys stopped performing and it broke Betty's heart. She'd been trying to persuade them to do a show for the partygoers tonight – a friendly crowd, people who loved them.

"Just think about it," she said. "Don't rule it out."

Ollie and Max didn't turn their heads from their program.

"I miss how they used to be," Betty whispered. Midge gave her a tight smile and she realized it had come out wrong. Max had scars on his face from when he'd walked through a glass door three years earlier, faded but still red. He couldn't handle the burden of being a freak magician on top of it. Betty searched for redirection. "Are you bringing champagne?" she asked.

Midge loosened. "Three bottles. On ice. What else can we bring?"

"Just yourselves. We've got beer, wine, rum, a full bar. Owen Appelbaum's going to bartend. Robert's out buying crab for dinner now. We're just going to graze all night."

"I can't remember the last time I had crabs," Midge said.

"That's good," said Betty. "Keep it that way."

Later, Betty salted the water and lifted the crabs from the cooler. One took a swipe at her as she dropped it into the giant stock pot at a rolling boil. She watched it slowly turn from blue to red. Finally, it floated to the top. Betty poked at the brine.

By ten o'clock, everyone was drunk. Betty hadn't planned on the crabs being so hard to eat. The nutcrackers left jagged points of shell that everyone had to pick and suck at to get to the meat, which was so watery it did almost nothing to slow the alcohol as it washed down their throats. Kenneth, who lived three doors down, sat cross-legged on the floor beside a man Betty suspected was his boyfriend. Kenneth's fingers bled from broken shell shards and the two men rocked in hysterics. Owen poured drinks from behind a long folding table they'd set up as a bar, accompanied by a pretty blonde woman he'd introduced to Betty as his girlfriend, Hannah. The two of them played gin rummy with each other in between pours. Owen lived three doors down in a house he'd inherited when his mom died, and Kenneth lived in a yellow bungalow at the neck of the cul-de-sac, where he hosted Dungeons and Dragons games on Friday nights. Betty and Robert had been invited a few times but it was not their scene, to put it mildly. Betty didn't actually know how one played Dungeons and Dragons, but she imagined it involved wearing costumes and acting out fantasies. No, thank you. She wondered if Owen and this new girlfriend joined them.

The only sober people she could find tonight were the kids. Ollie and Max sat at the kitchen table catapulting olives with a fork over a moat they'd made from plastic cups filled with water. Betty almost asked if they were going to do their show but thought better of it. She stood in the kitchen doorway and watched as they propelled olives at an unseen enemy.

"Yes, we're going to pick up the olives, Mom," Ollie said, without turning his head to see her, without her having made a sound.

"Where I'm from we used to call a dress like that a little slip of a thing," Milt said. Betty hadn't heard him approach. She'd taken Midge's advice and cleaned up after all, and wore a black cocktail dress that came just above the knee with a floral cut-out pattern over sheer dark silk and a slyly plunging neckline. Midge was right. Betty hadn't worn the dress in years but now remembered that people were always nicer to her when she did. They smiled more and seemed more interested in what she had to say.

Milt held a Manhattan in his hand with a curled lemon rind on the edge. She smelled whiskey on his breath.

"Happy New Year, Milt." Betty raised her glass and they clinked.

"I think my wife is getting tipsy," he said, pointing with his chin. Robert and Midge sat on the piano bench in the living room.

Robert had told Midge some kind of joke and Midge was buckled with the giggles.

"That's my fault," said Betty. "I screwed up the food. And Robert didn't buy enough bread."

"We've got a Y2K survival box in our garage," said Milt. "Want me to go get it? It's got turkey jerky and granola bars."

Betty smiled. "Let's see how we do. We might need it later."

Midge waved them over and Milt and Betty joined the two of them. Midge put her hand heavily on Betty's arm. "Robert has tequila he brought back from Mexico he says is so good it tastes like brandy. We're going to drink it."

"I thought you were saving that," Betty said.

Robert looked jaunty, loose. "I was," he answered. "Saving it for tonight." He held the bottle by the neck. He poured a splash in Midge's glass and then into Milt and Betty's once they'd emptied what they had. "To Betty and to Midge," Robert said, raising his glass high. "To the mothers."

The mothers. What was that supposed to mean? They clinked. "To the mothers," they answered.

"So, you got this in Mexico?" Milt said, taking a slug of his drink. "That's not a bad gig you have. Hopping to Mexico to buy tequila and write about what time the bars close. Beats going to an office."

Robert smiled coolly. "Travel writing is a bit more than tracking bar hours. But seeing the world from new perspectives does beat the nine to five, you're right about that."

"Oh, sure," said Milt. "I cast no aspersions. But I mean, it's not like you're a war correspondent." He laughed. "It's tourism. It's seeing the world through tourists' eyes."

"Travel is not the same thing as tourism," corrected Robert. "Tourism is going to Cabo and thinking you know Mexican culture.

Travel is talking to the locals and finding out how they live."

Milt snorted. "I think that's anthropology. I'm not being rude here. I'm just saying you write guidebooks for people to take on vacation. People need guidebooks. It's not a criticism."

Betty looked around to see if anyone else was hearing this. People were laughing and talking with each other; no one was looking at them. The room was spinning just the smallest bit.

"I'm pretty sure that's a criticism," said Robert. "But that's okay. You're a guest in our home. You get to say whatever the fuck you want tonight."

"Robert," said Betty. "Relax, honey."

"Me? I'm relaxed," said Robert. His hand bobbled as he poured himself more tequila. "I'm just trying to figure out which asshole this guy is shitting out of."

"Robert!" Betty said. Robert tottered on his feet and grinned.

"Milt," Midge said to her husband placatingly, "Robert writes books. He's a writer. Like Betty."

Robert laughed at this.

Betty had seen her husband drunk a hundred times. He was not a mean drunk. They were riding off into the weeds tonight and she did not know why.

"You know," said Midge, "this really does taste like brandy."

"Right?" said Robert. "They call it the pearl of tequilas."

Betty was grateful for Midge's rescue. "Isn't it weird to think a pearl is just an irritant that an oyster spends its life smoothing out to make it stop hurting?" said Betty. She had read this in a magazine.

"You're a crack up," said Midge.

Robert raised his glass to his wife. "Don't ever change, my dear."

Betty opened the sliding glass door to get some air. She felt jangly, askew. Maybe the doomsday hecklers were right – maybe there was a pressure in the atmosphere.

She belched and felt a creeping nausea, and for a flash instant wondered if she was pregnant. It was impossible, she knew that. She and Robert hadn't had sex in months and besides, she was barely getting periods anymore. Still, it was the same flutter she'd felt with Abby and Ollie. She took a deep breath.

Alice Pippick, Midge and Milt's youngest, sat on the patio with Nunkin on her lap. All by herself. Alice was eleven now – was she even old enough to stay awake till midnight? Should she even be here?

"Hi honey," Betty said, walking over. "Are you having fun?"

"Sure," the girl said.

"Don't you want to play with the boys?"

Alice ignored her.

Eleven. The same age Abby had been the last time Betty understood her own daughter. After that, Betty was always saying or doing the wrong thing, failure after failure. Abby had had a fitful adolescence, each year growing harder to decipher. Betty tried not to take it personally, but after enough times getting shut down, she started to resent it. At some point it just wasn't fair.

She looked up at the stars. "Sometimes it's nice to be alone at a party, too." She sat down beside her. "You know, this view reminds me of a place called Echo Canyon I used to go to with my grandpa growing up. How it curves around the houses."

Alice turned. "It doesn't curve around the houses," she said.

"Of course it does," said Betty. This was just plain fact. It wasn't some fuzzy opinion. An anger rose inside her. Why did people not accept any God damn thing she said? Betty was not speaking in tongues. She was not a hard person to understand. In the darkness she couldn't prove the shape of the canyon that they all saw every single day, but for Christ's sake.

Betty finished her tequila. "How did Nunkin get in here anyway? I filled the hole he dug."

"I don't know," said Alice. "He was just here."

Betty made a commitment to herself not to take out her annoyance on a child. The two sat in silence for a while looking at shadows playing against the trees and hearing murmurs coming from the party. Alice stroked Nunkin's head. Betty felt tired, leaden in her chair. It was after eleven now; she wasn't sure she'd make it until midnight. Milt's voice resonated through the glass as he held court, and she heard the dips and peaks of laughter and conversation.

"I'm gonna take Nunky home, hon," Betty said. "Can I have him?"

Alice handed up the dog, who roused from his contented stupor. "Do you have everything you need here?" Betty asked.

Again, Alice simply did not answer. Betty stood there, flummoxed by this breach of social contract. Someone speaks to you, you answer. My God, she thought, anger blooming again so fast.

"You're hurting Nunkin," Alice said, and Betty realized she was clenching him. She loosened her grip but was speechless. She left the girl to whatever universe she lived in and trod around the side of her house to Midge's.

The front door was unlocked, as always. Betty turned the handle and stepped inside. "Okay, Nunky. You stay here, you got it?" She bent down and placed the dog on the carpet. Nunkin leapt from her arms and shot up the stairs like a bullet. Once again, Betty felt unmoored. There was no reason the dog couldn't go upstairs, but why run like that?

She tried to hear what he was doing. She heard shuffling, movement. There was something going on up there. She narrowed her eyes and listened.

She had no plan but felt her body gliding up the stairs. Betty's heart thumped. Her eye twitched. The nausea was back, tickling her throat. She crept down the darkened hallway. The bedroom door was ajar and a honeyed light leaked out. She heard muted voices and pushed open the door.

There she saw him, the lines of his body so familiar. The bend of his elbow; the arch of his spine. His glossy hair obscured his face, loosely covering his eyes. The soft, round moons of his buttocks rose and fell, pushing down between the splayed legs of Midge Pippick.

Midge lolled her head toward Betty and stared drunkenly. Nunkin jostled against Betty's ankles as he scampered out.

"You're green," Midge said.

"I'm green?" Robert asked. He groaned and moaned.

"Not you," Midge answered. "Betty."

It's true what they say, thought Betty. Your life does flash before your eyes. She saw it all recalibrate, clicking into place: Robert's delightful curiosity, sated years before he found the nuggets Betty felt were still within her to be surfaced. How he loved the *idea* of her, but not quite the real person, though until now she herself could not have explained the difference. All the years of asking for permission to exist, over and over and over, without realizing she was talking only to herself. She saw it all in the undulating orbs of Robert's bottom.

Robert locked eyes with his wife, his body still thrusting.

Betty opened her mouth to speak, to tell them everything. Her stomach lurched. Her head rocked back and roared forward, vomit firing from the depths of her belly. Betty was a fountain, a spewing cherub, a she-devil. Robert and Midge screamed and tried to roll away but got tangled in the twisted bedsheets. Pink crab awash in frothy bile splattered on their naked bodies.

Betty staggered to the balcony and hung her head over the side. She heard them stumble to the bathroom. She wiped her mouth with the back of her hand. Her nose ran, her eyes stung. The night was crisp against her dampened skin. She felt clean and emptied.

From Midge's balcony she could see her own house below, hear voices rising from the party. Through the glass she saw Ollie and Max in full regalia. Ollie wore a top hat and gestured with a white-tipped wand while Max held up a red cape. The party guests surrounded them, enthralled. She saw Nunkin scarfing crumbs off the floor under the table like a tiny starving pig. The show ended and the crowd began the midnight countdown.

Betty stood upright and looked into the moonlit canyon. She was struck dumb by what she saw. Alice had been right. From here, it was clear the ravine opened up beyond her yard and spread out into a wide and shallow basin. It didn't curve around the houses at all. What she thought had been a canyon all these years was really just a shrubby pocket.

Hello, thought Betty. *Where are you. I am here.* No one answered. How could she have missed this.

THE THINGS YOU PREPARE FOR

Jessie had green eyes and wavy hair, and while she was slender, her body was more lanky than pert or curvaceous. Her attractiveness was so profound, though, it was more like a scent. The dullest, rattiest sweatshirt would hang from her body with such effortlessness it became beautiful. When she listened it was with intensity, punctuated by warm laughter and a brush of her fingers against your arm.

We lived on the same hallway our freshman year at UNH. Jessie and Ezra dated from the start; I was *Zinger* (never Abby – they always called me by my last name), the Best Friend. I was a third wheel, but it wasn't as bad as it sounds. Jess was like a secret pass to the world: even sitting with her in the library was festive, knowing I had been singled out to be there. We passed notes in class, and late at night we'd stumble to the after-hours cafe and eat calzones. Some weekends the three of us would drive from Durham into Boston and wander around Quincy Market. Ezra would buy us fistfuls of flowers at the farmers market. On nights when we'd have too much to drink I would stay in Jessie's room, sleeping on the floor while the two of them curled up above me in her single bed. We'd all go to breakfast in the morning. I didn't know which one of them I loved more.

Because I came from out of state, my reputation didn't precede

me. Fancy that. We never talked about it and it became clear early
on that they thought I was naive. I did not, let's say, redirect their
supposition. I didn't tell them about Ennis, the chunky wrestler
who was so muscular it strained my neck to rest my head on his
chest. Or Hector, who wore his grandfather's watch. Vinny, who
I found rifling through my desk drawer when I came out of the
bathroom. I didn't bring up the tricky day in high school when
I took too many pills. My new start with them felt glorious.
I wanted things before I met them, that's what I'm trying to get
at. I was jangly elbows and buck teeth and desire. I waited for the
right time to tell them all about it, but the right time never came.

I dated, but I never got invested. Ezra bought me drinks after
the breakups and would say he didn't know why I didn't have
a dozen suitors lined up at my door. I took the drinks, and the
compliments. I was like a sister to him, or a brother. I knew he
loved me, as much as you can love someone whom you also per-
ceive to be invisible.

After college we all ended up in San Francisco, not far from
San Encanto, the suburb where I grew up. I got a studio apartment
in the Mission and they lived nearby in Noe Valley. I temped at
a company that made motivational and inspirational posters, Jessie
worked as a nanny for two little girls, and Ezra transcribed meeting notes for a corporate law office while he went to law school.
One December evening when Jessie was in Laconia visiting her
parents, I went with Ezra to his office holiday party. We sat in
a cubicle drinking warm eggnog and talking. I'd been having an
awful winter. I couldn't stop worrying about things. I'd lie awake
at night and listen for the neighbors, who cursed at their children.
When it rained, I thought about all the animals outside in the cold.

Tornadoes crashed through the Midwest; the space shuttle tumbled into Texas. It was all I could do to keep track of it.

"The bad things that happen are never the things you prepare for," I told Ezra. He was unusually attentive to me that night. He sat forward and nodded.

"Don't worry about people. People are fine, Zinger," he said.

"They're not, though," I countered. "There are disasters happening constantly. We just never hear about them."

Ezra went and got me another eggnog. "I feel like you're a nurse," I said when he came back, "and I'm a burn victim. Like Juliette Binoche and that guy in *The English Patient*. You're ministering to me, giving me liquids through a crackly hole in my scabby face."

"Sip," he said, raising the eggnog to my lips.

Outside, we waited for a taxi. I shivered under a light winter coat. He took out a cigarette and lit it, not taking the match from the book before striking it. "Want one?" he teased, knowing I didn't smoke.

He inhaled deeply and blew the smoke in rings.

"Yes, actually," I said. "Can I have one?"

He smiled and lit me a cigarette from his own, then gave it to me. The filter was still damp from his saliva when I put it in my mouth. I inhaled and immediately felt a head rush like I had in high school, smoking for the first time.

"I think I've had too much eggnog tonight and not enough to eat," I said. "This is making me feel lightheaded."

He put his arm around me. "You need to get out more, friend," he said.

A cab went by and I raised my hand at it, but it was full. We stood there, leaning against each other.

"You know what you need, Zinger?" he said.

"No, tell me."

"You need to do more drugs. Have you ever done ecstasy? You would love ecstasy."

"I don't want to do ecstasy. I don't need to feel any less in control than I do already," I said.

"You and I should do ecstasy some time. Ecstasy would be perfect for you."

"You think that, even with your brother?" I asked.

"Rafy's fine," he said. "Don't believe the hype."

Rafy, with his slight frame and confusing eyes. On a permanent high since he took bad LSD at fourteen. That's why Ezra was in law school. Rafy's darting eyes meant that Ezra was the only one who could take over the family practice. Never mind that he wanted to be a river guide. Rafy was sick, his sister was a flake, so it fell to him. A good person, Ezra did not tell them no. His no's leaked out in other ways.

"I have some ecstasy in my apartment," he said. "Come over. You'll forget all about this crap. You'll be a whole new woman."

"What if I like the woman I already am?" I asked.

He dropped his cigarette onto the sidewalk and looked at me. "Do you?"

A cab pulled up. Ezra opened the door. He got in and closed the door behind us. He hugged me. "You won't regret this, Abby," he said.

We drove in silence for several blocks, snug against each other. I stared out the window, looking up at the moon. We passed the streetlit businesses and partiers out for the night. We passed the power plant, all wires and electrical fences. I remembered riding in a car with Alex, a guy I had gone out with at UNH.

"When we broke up, Alex said he wanted to crash into a place like this and kill himself," I said. Not my best timing.

When Ezra put his hand on my leg, just above the knee, at first I thought it was an accident. Slowly, he began tracing his fingers in tiny circles. I stared dumbly at my thigh and his thick fingers.

"Can I ask you a question?" he said.

"What," I said.

"Are we *ever* going to kiss?"

Though it was he who was making the pass, I felt caught in my secret attraction.

"What about Jess?"

He waved his hand dismissively. "I'm not saying we should fuck," he said. The taxi driver's eyes flashed in the rearview mirror. "I just thought we should kiss."

"I don't know," I said.

But I did know. I didn't move. I didn't say yes. I stayed still just long enough for the decision to be his, which is a decision in and of itself, I realize, but an easier one to live with.

I thought it would be a peck, an exploratory smack, but he went at me with gusto, his tongue in my mouth, his body leaning against mine and pushing me down into the seat. I heard my bag slide onto the floor and my keys fall out. Dirt and lint pressed against my cheek. And yet – I saw stars. There on the tacky back seat, I was drifting into outer space, the whole starry universe unfolding.

"Wait," I said.

He stopped. He sat up and took my hand. "I'm sorry," he said.

"It's okay," I said. He stroked the back of my hand.

When the cab arrived at my apartment I got out. Ezra raised his palm in a wave and the cab rattled away. I stood there in the clear night air beneath the moon. What do people do when they have these feelings? Where do they keep them?

Jessie brought me pears in a brown paper bag the day she got back. I brought them into the kitchen. They were round, firm, perfect. I washed one at the sink and bit into it and the juice dripped into my sleeve. As it did, memories of Alex flooded back to me. We had met at a party. Alex walked up to me with a red beer cup in his hand. "Abby, right?" he said. "You're in my Poli Sci class." He had a pleasant scent, warm and musky underneath his argyle sweater. We both looked over at Jessie. She sat with Ezra in the corner, leaning close as if she'd known him for a thousand years. And Alex said, "So what's it like having a beautiful best friend?"

What's it like?

I smiled like he was flirting with me. "It's fun," I said.

And then I dated that guy. I dated him.

Jessie came in as I wiped my hand on my jeans.

"Your chin is peeling," she said. I touched it. Dry from where Ezra's whiskers had rubbed against it.

"Huh," I said. "I'm using a new astringent. I guess it's too strong."

"Try witch hazel," she said.

"I will," I said.

"You should."

"I will," I repeated.

"It's gentle, and it's natural."

"For fuck's sake, Jess, let it go," I said. Hurt shadowed her face, and I regret that. I softened. "It's okay," I told her. "I'll deal with it."

Does she really need every last star?

GIUSEPPE AND EMILINE

Giuseppe came to Emiline from above. He was round as a hot air balloon but heavy as a walrus, with little flipper feet and tiny hands flapping out from his sides. He descended upon her from the sky, darkening out the daylight above her, waving his stubby arms and feet as his balloon-body glided earthward, until he alit, square on top of her, and let out a satisfied sigh of relief.

"Oh," Emiline cried. He sat on her back, squashing her face into the sidewalk. The pavement scratched at her and a pebble dug into her cheek. "Get up, Giuseppe!" she wailed. "You're crushing me! I can't breathe!"

Giuseppe rolled around on top of her, reveling in the softness of his landing. Emiline dragged her fingernails along the pavement and kicked her feet in the air, but if he knew that he had landed on her, Giuseppe did not care.

Emiline married Giuseppe because she loved him like a brother, the brother she had always longed for when she was a girl. She had grown up by herself, an only child to parents who worked at the university laboratory and came home and buried themselves under the papers on their desks, piled as high as haystacks. Emiline would knock on their study door. She could hear the papers rustle.

"Come in!" her mother would cry. Emiline would peer around the heavy oaken door. She'd see a hand clutching eyeglasses sticking out amid the heap of manuscripts and data tables, or perhaps she would find her father's shoe, kicked off and thrown across the room.

"Do I disturb you?" Emiline would ask.

"Of course not, dear," her mother would answer. "Did you finish your dinner?"

"Yes," Emiline would lie. She hadn't finished her dinner. She'd fed it to her imaginary brother and saved the cold bits for herself.

"Hand me my cup of tea, would you, darling?"

Emiline would push the teacup and saucer closer to the large pile, while her mother's delicate hand waved blindly.

"Thank you, dear," said her mother, curling a long finger around the teacup's ear-shaped grasp.

Emiline withdrew to bed.

When Emiline met Giuseppe, he was the first person who had ever listened to her. He used to tell her, "I want to know everything about you. Are you hot, are you cold? I want to know. Are you frightened? What did you have for breakfast?"

"I had oatmeal, with almonds and sunflower seeds," Emiline would tell him.

"Sunflower seeds!" Giuseppe would proclaim. "My sunflower. You shine with a brilliance few women will ever know."

There was more. He liked to brush Emiline's hair, plucking out the burrs and stickums that had landed there during the day, working out the knots with warm oil. His hands were strong, and sometimes he would stroke his thumbs along the nape of her neck until she felt herself surrender.

He had a big walnut bed with a patchwork quilt and flannel sheets, and Emiline liked to burrow herself there, watching the dust motes dance in a strip of morning light that cut through the room and landed in a shiny pool on her jacket, which she sometimes dropped on the floor.

They had a small wedding in the back room of the courthouse. Giuseppe's large family, whom Emiline had never met before and hadn't seen since, spilled out into the aisles and jostled each other for the best view of the bride and groom, taking photographs and murmuring with approval to each other as Giuseppe and Emiline exchanged vows.

For fourteen months, Emiline was content. Giuseppe worked at his pizzeria and brought her flowers on Friday afternoons, usually posies and snapdragons but sometimes yellow daisies. Emiline made shepherd's pie and goulash and casseroles that filled both of them up and usually put Giuseppe to sleep, head on the table.

Shortly after their first anniversary, though, things began to change. First of all, Giuseppe began to grow. Each breath he took sucked up more air. His hands became wider until his wedding ring would not come off, but gripped his finger like a tiny gold vise. When they went out to eat, Giuseppe took up almost all of Emiline's field of vision as she sat opposite him at the table.

Maybe it was the casseroles, or maybe it was some kind of an illusion, because he only seemed to grow large on certain days of the week. If Emiline looked at him suddenly, turned her head too quickly, he appeared bloated, puffy, his feet even floating a bit above the ground. If she turned her head slowly, and crept a glance at him quietly, there was Giuseppe, back to his usual size, polishing the silverware and whistling a small tune.

Not long thereafter, Emiline began to feel as if she was being followed. Shadows in the alleyways reached out to her on the street, but she never found anyone there.

One day, instead of looking over her shoulder, Emiline looked up. And there he was. A dirigible in the sky. She squinted at him, covering her eyes from the bright sun, but she was certain of it. Giuseppe floated high above her, coasting along in the summer breeze.

Day after day, it went on like this. In the grocery store, she'd feel his presence, and catch a glimpse of him hovering outside when she passed the window by the mangoes and kumquats. Giuseppe trailed her on her errands, blotting out the sun, and when she stopped and had tea at a cafe, he shaded her newspaper and cooled the afternoon heat with his overbearing girth.

Some days, he would swoop down and land on her without warning, his shadow blossoming in size as he tumbled. She would try to run but he came too quickly and he would crush her, pinning her to the sidewalk, scraping her cheeks and giving her bruises on her arms and legs. The mangoes and kumquats would roll into the gutter.

No one seemed to notice, though a little white dog tied to a post once barked wildly.

When she came home, he would be there, the man she knew, whistling as he chopped the onions and poured the evening wine. She peered at him sideways, still tingling from the scratches and sidewalk burns.

He'd hand her a goblet of wine with a smile and a wink. Emiline looked at his hands, smooth and graceful, no longer bloated like water balloons. She drank her wine.

She vowed that she would talk to him about it. But every time the moment seemed right, she would open her mouth, timidly,

fish-like, and before she could speak, Giuseppe would take up all
the air. "You're my idol, baby," he would say. "Have I ever told you
that? Every man on the street is jealous because I'm walking next
to such a fine young thing. I dig that, Emiline. I dig you, and I dig
that."

Giuseppe stabbed radicchio and arugula drenched in olive oil
and stuffed it in his mouth, salad dressing running down his chin in
a rivulet that forked into a Y and then dripped onto the tablecloth.

Emiline's fish mouth closed. Opened. Closed.

Nighttimes were the worst. She would dream of her parents,
now long dead, and her imaginary brother, long dead, too. How
terribly she missed them. Emiline didn't want Giuseppe's posies,
or his snapdragons. She wanted to go home.

Emiline lay in bed looking at the ceiling and listened to
Giuseppe's heavy, labored breathing, remnants of the evening's goulash rattling around in his throat. She knew that in the morning
the slice of light would cascade through the split in the curtains,
decorating a shimmering wall between the window and the bed.
She closed her eyes and looked forward to that.

Giuseppe stirred. He clattered his throat and sniffled. He
smacked his heavy lips. Emiline kept her eyes closed and imagined
the golden wall of light, dancing for her in the morning.

The bed creaked and moaned and shifted, and Giuseppe rolled
his walrus body on top of her. Emiline opened her eyes and turned
her head to the window, searching for a sign.

But Giuseppe raised himself above her, and the moonlight
disappeared.

CROSSING LOG

7:02   Gert Rosenblatt, signing in.

7:04   Walk to position on corner. Temp is approx. 71 degrees; warm. Put on orange reflective jacket and crossing guard smock; assess area. No cars in drop-off zone; one brown car parked kitty corner from school with driver waiting. No visible children. Do not believe my five-minute late arrival has had negative impact, though I note it here per Barry's instrux. Understand lateness not okay; extenuating circumstances include difficulty accessing bathroom (Gebhardt had morning tummy trouble, nothing serious), late bus (I was on time), and turning back to retrieve pistachios inadvertently left at home. Need protein to prevent low blood sugar during morning hours, esp. with high morning sun. Acknowledge "no excuses" policy per Barry; noting that this is not excuse, but rather further information re: arrival time, which did not have negative impact on any children.

7:06   Wave at passing cars in greeting.

7:07   Escort two children and one adult across street. Believe girls are Shari and Kari Sperber. Cannot tell S and K apart; both wear hair in two braids and have pink jacket. Mother Sperber talking on phone while crossing street, not watching children nor autos. I relate to her that I am extra security for children, not replacement for parental supervision. Mother Sperber immersed in call, does not reply, though turns head after safe passage across street.

7:10   No children.

7:13   Major influx of children. Six children; two adults. Two boys are engaged in physical combat while waiting to cross. Mother separates boys. I withhold passage to the group until boys have calmed down. Second adult circumvents my authority and crosses street with three children. I blow whistle and alert her I am recording their actions. No deterrent. Recording action, per warning.

7:15   Single child, unattended.

7:17   No children. Pistachio break. Noting instrux not to bring food on job. Understand re: candy, large meals, but protein hit seems reasonable. Barry sez no, not for 45-minute shift. Gebhardt sez not legal; sez suable offense, but don't want to sue. Not threatening legal action. Not being difficult, per Barry's warning. Only noting need for protein hit in log.

7:24   Set up portable walker seat for temporary rest. Acknowledge against rules per Barry's note, but no children visible and do not understand requirement to stand when no action to be taken. Finished bag of pistachios, weighing thirst vs. hunger; remembered salt is lost thru sweat and pistachios are salted, tipping balance.

7:35   Regret pistachios. Thirsty.

7:40   Desmond Swartzman and mother arrive; cross when there
is a break in cars but in advance of my directive. Swartzman mother
uses obscenity at me when I cry "Halt!" and blow whistle. *Repeat*:
Swartzman mother uses obscenity at me when I cry "Halt!" and
blow whistle. Desmond raised middle finger at me upon arrival to
other side of street, with no visible consequence from parent. Do
not understand how parents cannot realize that children learn by
our actions. Desmond is child. Concerned Desmond will not turn
out to be reasonable, kind, safe member of society when parental
modeling includes disrespectful behavior and language. Concerned
about how rest of year will go if parental frustrations are so high
already. Understand need for two-income households (I am working; I understand financial pressures; Gebhardt is the one not
working [not a prob.]; do not have issue with working mothers)
but working mothers do not need to take out frustrations on service personnel trying to help them; i.e., me.

7:42   Driver exits brown car across street. Approaches.

7:59   Please excuse missing time in log. Barry's notes from
exchange will reflect time block, though will likely not correspond
to my record of events here. Reiterating: understand rules against
sitting; eating; prompt arrival; no more conflict with parents or
children; use of whistle only in emergency; "no excuses" policy.
Reasonable explanations for exceptions to all of the above noted
in this log. Further, spying is demoralizing; not wise management
practice. Told Barry I would appeal firing to school board and do
not believe his assertion that school board authorized it. Returned

orange reflective jacket, crossing guard smock and stop sign, per his demand. Washed my face in girls' bathroom (still hot). Phoned Gebhardt from front office and he says Barry was forty miles of bad road from Day One, and we will fight this.

8:02   School bell rings. Children safely rendered into classrooms. Hallways quiet.

Exit Strategies

You meet Reggie at your temp job at the poster company. You file invoices by color and by number. He does data entry at the workstation behind the receptionist. He appeared there one day, his fingers typing softly while your supervisor, Elaine, leaned next to him, talking quietly. She asked you for a pencil at one point, and you gave one to her.

Reggie's hair is blond and straight and a little stringy, and his body is thin and tan. You take him to be a surfer, and half-expect to see puka shells around his neck. His teeth are small and a little gray and they remind you of a hamster or a cartoon woodchuck. You imagine him gnawing rapid-fire on a log with them, making a dam or a log cabin.

Yet you feel drawn to him. You can almost feel static electricity rise up from the carpet through your legs as you pass his workstation, his back turned and arms moving quietly on the keyboard. When you finally meet in the kitchen on his third day there, you know he feels it, too. Your hands fumble with coffee spoons and water bottles. Your small talk makes no sense. You know that you are sweating, even though you put on baby powder so you won't have to spend as much on dry cleaning. But today you are nervous and your left armpit has broken through, sweat trickling down your side in a cool rivulet, leaving a mark as big as a Danish pastry.

One day, Reggie asks you if you want to ride your bicycle with him on National Bike to Work Day, a holiday you had not known existed. City riding terrifies you, and you aren't that adept on a bicycle in the best of circumstances. You always grip the handlebars too tightly and startle easily. You agree to do it.

He comes by your house that morning, wearing shiny blue cycling shorts and wrap-around sunglasses. You are nervous so he insists on riding behind you to make sure you are okay. It mortifies you to think of him watching you in an unglamorous hunch, your ass bouncing over every pothole.

It doesn't matter. At Third and Mission your bike chain comes off and Reggie stops and manipulates it back on, gently tugging and sliding it until his hands are covered with black grease. As he kneels on the pavement at your feet, you feel stunned by the solicitude of his pose. He stands up and flashes his gray little teeth at you, like a child's smile, giddy. He kisses you quickly and gets back onto his bike.

On the ride home you stop at a bar and you both get staggering drunk, giggling and swaying in your seats. You go to the bathroom at one point and look deep into your own eyes in the mirror, but you're too drunk to figure out what question you're hoping to answer. You wipe a bread crumb from your cheek instead.

That night, you spend the night at his house, a railroad Victorian on Valencia with bicycles belonging to all his roommates lining the narrow hallway. You wash your face with his hand soap and brush your teeth with your fingers. When you come into his bedroom, he is already naked under the covers. You slip out of your clothes while he watches. You leave your underwear on, and then take it off once you are in bed.

You trace your hand along the puffy ridge at Reggie's cheekbone, below the socket of his eye. His whiskers stop, and the skin is perfectly smooth. He runs his fingers through your hair, and you kiss for a few minutes. And you learn that Reggie is a wet kisser. His tongue comes out, and it sweeps around in your mouth like a radar. At one point, he hooks his finger on your lower teeth and holds your mouth open as he wags his tongue back and forth. It leaves you wide-eyed and speechless.

"Did I mention," Reggie whispers, "that I've never been able to sustain a relationship for longer than three months?"

You think he is making a joke. "Why do you think that is?" you ask him.

"I don't know," he says warmly. "Short attention span, I guess."

Reggie is your seventh boyfriend. You have slept with four of them and gotten naked with two. The last one broke up with you, which surprised you, since you are usually the one plotting exit strategies.

On Valentine's Day, Reggie gives you a drawing of a heart he made with crayons and your name, which he spells "Abbie," written in glitter glue. You have made nothing for him. He says, "You can make it up to me later," in a suggestive way. Five years from now you will remember this moment as the first time you really felt like an adult. Five years after that, you will realize that this is pathetic. But for now, you grasp the Valentine and try not to smudge the corners, knowing you will never throw it away.

But just as he predicted, nearly three months later, Reggie starts getting tired of you. You begin to have a harder time getting his attention. His eyes wander and he multitasks when you talk to him. He starts to harbor small frustrations with you – the way you eat your food (too slowly), the way you fold your clothes when you're

at the laundromat together (too precisely), the way you have to fill
the silences with questions. "Nothing bad will happen in a silence,"
he tells you one night as you walk home from La Cumbre Taqueria.
"I know," you answer, lying. You walk a few more minutes until you
can't bear it any longer, and you blurt out, "It's a beautiful night,
isn't it?" Reggie doesn't answer.

The end comes one day when you are standing in the lobby of
Japantown Center waiting for Reggie to see a matinee of *Sideways*.
You are seventeen minutes early. When Reggie arrives, you can tell
by the expression on his face that he is mad at you. He doesn't stop
to greet you, but instead keeps walking and says, "Come on, let's
go," as he passes. You skitter along a step behind him as you walk
toward the cinema. "Why are you always early?" he says to you, over
his shoulder.

"I don't know," you answer. "The early bird gets the worm?"

"I feel like you're always rushing me," he says.

"I'm sorry," you say to the back of his head. "Slow down."

But he doesn't. He keeps going. "The early bird doesn't get the
worm," he says. "The early bird eats alone and then sits around
waiting for the other birds to get there, and then makes them all
feel guilty."

Afterwards, when you are sitting in the car on your street, you
ask him what's the matter. You say it in a sheepish voice, like a little
girl. You think you are annoying, an annoying person, and you wish
someone would put you out, like a cigarette, or a pet. Or make you
disappear, like your brother Ollie used to do in his magic tricks.
Reggie turns his head and looks out the window. You watch the skin
pull taut over his Adam's apple, stubble and red bumps on his neck.

"*How* am I pressuring you?" you ask, hearing your own childlike
whine.

"The fact that you don't know just proves my point," Reggie says, turning to face you.

You pull yourself together. "Okay," you say with a flatness. "Why don't you give me a call later, if you feel like it."

"Okay, babe," he says, relieved, and handsome again.

You walk down the street toward your apartment, hearing the soles of your shoes slap against the pavement. It's almost five o'clock. The sky is turning purple. It is mottled with ruby clouds. It's a bruise the size of the universe.

Although you do not love Reggie, it will take you two years to get over him, and six years before you can no longer remember why he made you feel so bad. Until the day you learn your best friend is sick with cancer, you will always count this day as the worst one of your life. Later, you go through a phase when you recall him with affection, remember sitting on the hood of your car waiting for him to come downstairs to meet you, the nighttime breezes delicately wafting through your hair. And then one day you can't remember him, really, at all. Just the idea of him: that he was your seventh boyfriend; the one with blond hair; the one who lived on Valencia; the one you think of when you find a shoebox filled with tax receipts, old address books, and a heart-shaped Valentine.

RESURRECTION MAN

Battle of the Balls

Balls penetrate solid cups, vanish and reappear elsewhere. Need: cups, balls. AKA: Bean-sowing. Chop chop. The Old Army Game.

Tonight the asshole is sitting in the second row. He leans back in his chair, legs spread wide. He's on his fourth beer. Nightclubs are better than bachelorette booze cruises but every now and then a jerk comes in who wants to tear the magician down. It makes no sense – they buy the ticket, know what they're in for. Then they take each trick as a taunt. They are that insecure. And precisely because of this, Ollie knows what will shut them down. They wear their soft spots like armor.

This guy's weakness is that he loves his girlfriend and she does not love him. Ollie can see this from their body language. She sits upright but gentle, bows her head and smiles at Ollie, to compensate for her sloppy companion. The asshole hangs his head too, when he's not jutting his chin, because her disgust wounds him, though he doesn't know it yet. Two weeks or two months from now she'll be threatening to call the cops on him if he doesn't stop pounding on her door. But she hasn't found her voice yet, and he still thinks he can take care of her.

First come the interruptions. A muttered, "*It's a miracle!*" and then laughter at his own heckle. The girlfriend squirms. Ollie fans his cards along the felted table, looks directly at her and asks her to call out any card. "Nine of diamonds," she says softly. Ollie peers at the deck. "That's strange," he puzzles. "That card is missing." She gazes at him, eyes wet and unblinking. "Oh, wait." He pulls the card from his breast pocket. "Found it." He speaks only to her.

"*Bullshit!*" her companion coughs. Soon it will be disruptions, homophobic slurs. Too bad he's not doing the show with Max tonight. This only happens when he's solo. Phil is on security; Ollie can see he has his eye on the man. Phil will ask him to leave if he keeps it up, but by then it will be too late. It will be all anyone will remember.

Ollie looks down on the asshole with beneficence. "A non-believer. I feel you, my brother," he says. Then he nods toward the girlfriend. "She doesn't believe in *you*, either."

The audience laughs; someone calls out, "Burn!"

Ollie moves onto the next trick, Dodging a Bullet. The couple stays for a few minutes before her date tells her that it's time to go. She whispers in protest but he is already heading toward the door. So she collects her coat and hurries to the exit.

Ollie gets no joy from this. Well, of course he does, but he tries to avoid it when he can. The girl will have a bad night now. But he does her no favors by protecting her from the truth.

Our Little Secret

A bad hand turns into a good hand. Need: Standard deck of cards. AKA: Nothing Up My Sleeve; Ace in the Hole.

It's not that he can't hold down a job. It's that he has transferable skills and he applies them in multiple places. For a while, the car dealership seemed like the perfect fit: sales and magic are all about patter, relationships, transporting someone to a place where the world seems wondrous. What's more wondrous than a brand new car? Ollie can convince someone ice water can pour out of a raw egg, for Christ's sake. Selling cars is child's play.

A perennially cheerful man named Earl hires Ollie and Max as a team, because every good trick needs a distraction. Max is perfect for the role. He has scars on his face from a childhood accident and it throws customers off, so they overcompensate by opening up wider, lingering longer, letting down their guard, while Ollie sells them undercoat protection, extended warranties, ultra high-end rims.

They sell cars. Oh, they sell cars. They banter, make customers laugh, dazzle them with glinting, polished chrome and rich leather. The problem is, on the sales floor, no one delights at the moment they realize they've been fooled. They drive off with a brand new car, a lighter wallet, and a nagging realization that they've just been conned. Max and Ollie leave a wake of disgruntled customers, and one day Earl cheerfully encourages them to find another venue.

When they get jobs as poker dealers at Jack's 665 Club in San Encanto, for Ollie it's like sliding into soft socks that have been waiting for his aching feet his whole life. A homey little poker parlor exempt from zoning laws, the décor hasn't been updated in thirty years, save periodic refeltings. Ollie's father used to sneak out to play cards here when he was a kid, and now he can see why.

Occasionally a dabbler or new face might wander in, but it's mostly regulars. There's Bill, a decrepit old man who Jack comps dinner every night. There's Don, a greasy-haired cashier at the

7-Eleven; grouchy Ray is a guard at the county jail. Once a week, twice a week, or every night, depending on their paychecks and addictions. Jack walks the floor and counts the money and has known many of these people since high school.

Wednesday night is prime rib night; Thursdays are Seafood Special. Sunday night is Lingerie Ladies Night, when two ladies don sexy underwear and circle the tables with wicker baskets filled with bras and teddies and camisoles, under the pretense of selling them for the players' wives. The idea is absurd. Yet it's another one of Jack's traditions. No one knows whose idea it was when it started and no one will be the one to say it's time to end. Janine and Michelle sell a g-string or two and the tables are always fuller Sunday nights. No one complains, and no one asks Janine or Michelle what they do in their cars between shifts. It's family here.

Sandy tends the bar and serves the wedge potatoes (brought tableside so no one has to put down their cards to eat), and occasionally plays a hand when her shift is over. She's a lousy card player: she holds her breath whenever she has anything. Ollie hasn't had the heart to let her know she has a tell. Penny and Winter are dealers, firm but friendly, and they bitch about their kids and their exes when they smoke cigarettes in the parking lot on breaks.

It's a service, what this place does. Jack feeds these men (for they are mostly, but not all, men) the only hot meal they'll eat all day. Sees them more often than their wives and girlfriends. Notices when Bill seems out of sorts and calls his kids to let them know about it. He takes their money, yes, and it pays for vacations with his wife, and vacations with Penny on the side. No one turned away, except for lack of funds. Or cursing at the dealers. Or agitation when their luck won't turn around. Big Sammy sees those men out, though sometimes Jack follows in his car from a distance, just to make sure they get home safely. Like family.

Ollie loves it here. He gets free drinks on his breaks and a discount steak or basket of fried calamari for dinner. The work is easy: it's like doing magic tricks, without the magic tricks. Just deal, watch the table, tame the drunks, collect the chips. He could palm or count cards but there isn't any point; customers tip more when they win. "You've got a hand," he says to Bill, who falls asleep in between his turns. Bill jostles awake and looks at his cards. "You call this a hand?" he says, and tosses them face down on the table.

Tonight, Sandy pulls up a chair beside him and Ollie deals her in. It's getting late and some of the men are glassy-eyed, but no one is getting up. "Pot's light," Ollie says, nudging Bill. Bill blinks a couple times, peeks at his cards, and tosses in his bid. "Pot's right," says Ollie. He lays down the flop. King of clubs, four of clubs, ace of hearts. Sandy and Don and the others toss in their chips as it goes around the table, and then Bill raises and they go around again. Sandy hesitates when the bidding gets to her and she rechecks her cards, as she always does. She looks to Ollie and smiles, as if they've got a shared secret. He gives her a goofy grin back because Ollie has a tell, too – when he's near a woman he's in love with, he becomes a hopeless jackhole. With luck, the table hasn't seen it yet.

"Pot's right," Ollie says, and he deals the turn, and after that, the river. Not one player has folded. Grouchy Ray licks his lips and Sandy is breathing shallowly, but Ollie knows it's Bill's night to win the hand. Bill has breadcrumbs on his collar and his fingertips are damp and quavery against his martini glass. But Bill has been awake since he first glanced at his hand. Slumped, smacking his lips together softly, but very much awake and alive. Max has wandered over to the table and stands behind Ollie, resting a hand on his shoulder.

It's time for the showdown.

The Lady Disappears

A girl vanishes; only her clothes remain. Need: Black fabric backdrop with a slit; extra set of clothes; flash or bang. Also known as: Empty Pile of Clothes, Dress Hits Floor.

They are on a stage in an auditorium at a high school none of them attended. It's a Catholic school, with a giant parking lot and football field and three tennis courts. The nuns rent out the auditorium during the summer for forty bucks a night as a rehearsal space, so this is where Ollie, Max, and Sandy have come to raise the dead.

It will be his signature trick. *Resurrection Man.* He's been working on it for months. It's an old standard – a simple vanish and reproduction. But the lore behind it is what will be next-level. Resurrection Men who robbed graves and sold bodies to medical schools, quietly slipping corpses in through the back doors. Schools needed the cadavers for research. The law looked the other way. Digging up jewels, watches, wallets: that was a felony. Even if they got caught, taking bodies was a misdemeanor. What else could they do? How else would they be saved?

Ollie will be a modern-day Resurrection Man. He'll enthrall audiences with tales of empty graves, bodies rising up before the Final Judgment. The trick itself is simple: a warm body, delicate and alive, then a distraction, a quick slip-away behind a backdrop out of sightlines, and *poof!* Only clothes remain.

And yet it isn't working.

"You're overthinking this, baby," he tells Sandy, touching her chin with his fingers. Her skin is so soft. Now that she has moved in with him, all he wants is to fall asleep against her, go back to where they were this morning.

"I'm thinking, not overthinking," she says. "This is just the audience seeing a woman's red dress on the floor and imagining her naked. Ye Olde Male Fantasy."

"You don't see it. How can I make you see it?"

Max and Sandy share a look, as if Ollie isn't right in front of them.

"It's about free will, and mortality," Ollie says. "A second chance after a waking death. Don't you get it? It's a metaphor." He faces them on the flatly-lit stage.

"Resurrection," Max says. "I get it. The circle of life."

"Exactly," Ollie says. "Then *you* do it! You do the vanish." Max has been his magic partner since they were kids growing up on the same cul-de-sac. When they were twelve, they did shows at eight-year-olds' birthday parties. When they were eighteen, they busked on the street.

"I'm not a prop," says Max, "I'm a partner."

"Of course you are," says Ollie. He's missing the point.

"Besides," says Max, "how are we going to hide a second suit in my clothing? It's too bulky."

It isn't like Max to get caught up on solvable details. He doesn't want to do the trick. Ollie sits down on the floor, on blue painter's tape laid down from some teenage production.

Sandy and Max stand before him, their legs nearly touching. "This shouldn't be so hard," he says to their knees.

"Anyway," says Sandy from above him, "it's only resurrection if you bring the bodies back. How are you going to do that?"

Cornucopia

*The never-ending platter. Need: a picnic basket with a false side. Produce,
groceries, food. A tablecloth. Also known as: Horn of Plenty, Bottomless
Basket, Insatiable Appetite.*

Over the deli, there's wagon wheel next to a gigantic elk head. Or
a moose head – Ollie doesn't know. A huge head with antlers on
the wall. Ollie and Sandy are at the market by the Rushing River.
Sandy tears the list and hands half to him. "Meet at the front
when you're finished," she says, and walks toward an avalanche of
artisanal cheese.

Ollie looks at his list. Apple Cider Vinegar. Turkey Jerky. Face
masque. Is that like a mask you wear or the black lotion she puts on
her face at home? Why would she need that here? They never shop
like normal people. Sandy is always on some strange diet. They
never have anything to eat.

It's not really called the Rushing River. It's the Russian River.
But Sandy heard it as rushing the first time he said it, and why
wouldn't she? Who thinks of Russians when they think of rivers?
The ears hear what they expect. They had called it the Rushing
River ever since.

Through tinny loudspeakers, Patsy Cline is singing "Crazy,"
plaintive and heartbroken. It's like she knows she'll be dead at
thirty. Ollie leans on his cart and watches a woman at the deli case
who is way too friendly with the meat man. She wears big purple
glasses and beige polyester pants. "Hi, how are you!" she says to
him. "Guess who's not making dinner tonight!" She bobs on her
feet like she's dancing.

The deli man is bald, has a lightning bolt tattooed on his neck and a smooth, black crescent hooked through his earlobe. "I'm all right," he says warmly. Maybe he does know her. "I'm almost outta here so I can't complain."

Here is the trick he would do for the woman: Metamorphosis. A scarf becomes a dove becomes a rose she gets to keep. The illusion of courtship is what she wants: instant life change with no effort. And the guy? Money for Nothing, where his own twenty dollar bill keeps multiplying, pulled from every sleeve and cap, until it ends up back in his wallet, which, of course, it never left.

"Can I get the tiniest amount of that?" she asks him, pointing at the red pepper hummus. "It just looks too good to pass up." Three people stand behind her in a haphazard non-line, hard smiles straining their faces and their muscles ready to spring. The number system is out of tickets and they all think they are next. No tricks on them tonight.

Chocolate milk, rice milk, coconut milk, oat milk, milk in glass bottles. Whipping cream. Where is the regular milk? Ollie wonders. Who is this place for?

A man in a denim jacket and wire-rimmed glasses pushes by him with a cart that's empty, save two small children. Ollie sees Sandy up ahead in produce. This weekend away, it will help them. Sandy needs a change of scenery. She looks behind her for a second and then reaches in, plucks a grape, and pops it in her mouth. Jesus, Ollie laughs. Little criminal.

Tonight Ollie sees magic everywhere. Chakra candles offering money, love, health, confidence. Fake meat parading as real meat. The illusion of flesh. People want so badly to believe.

All the juices: carrot, coconut, blueberry, pomegranate, pear, papaya. Batteries, charcoal, paper plates. All the herbs and vitamins: cranberry, collagen, krill, little blue disks you stick under your

tongue. There's a bunch of condoms over the Tucks and Prepara-
tion H. Something called Jason with a line over the *a* and two dots
over the *o*. Baby food you squeeze from a tube.

"Put Your Head on My Shoulder" croons overhead now, and
Ollie circles the man with the kids in his cart for a second time.
Now there is a watermelon in the cart with them. Ollie sees families, pairs, singles, all pushing their carts down the aisles. It's like
they're on a loop. Garlic, habanero, jalapeno, avocado, guacamole.

The scene reminds him of his friend Bill, from the poker parlor,
who had to move into an old folks home that won't let him come
play poker anymore. He fell outside his condo by a planter box at
two in the morning coming home from Jack's and he couldn't get
himself back up. He lay on the cement pathway until dawn, when
a neighbor in monkey bedroom slippers and a bathrobe opened
her front door to get the paper. Ollie went to see Bill in the old
folks home. He snuck in a thermos of martinis. But Bill wasn't
in his room – it was 4:30, dinner time. So Ollie went down the
pastel hallway that had railings on each side until he got to the
dining hall, and was startled by the sight of maybe twenty walkers
parked outside the wide entrance. Some had green ribbons on the
handles and some had seats you could sit on, but all of them had
been abandoned at the door. It was as if the old people had been
raptured in their tracks.

Herring, tuna, canned crab, lobster pâté, smoked oysters. When
his parents got divorced, Ollie and his father ate smoked oysters
on Ritz crackers while they stood at the kitchen counter in his
dad's new apartment. Chewy, oily, buttery in his mouth. How old
was he, fifteen? Why is he thinking of this now? Why is he feeling
maudlin?

He rounds the corner and nearly collides with Sandy. She's

facing a wall of candy, a half-unwrapped chocolate bunny in her hands. She has bitten off its head and is eating slowly, gazing into the middle distance. So much for her supposed diet.

He taps her foot with the cart, grins, and says, "You're cheating!"

The color drains from her face. "No, I'm not," she says. Then, "Why would you even say that?"

Huh?

"I'm right here," Ollie says. "I can see you."

But then – oh. There it is. It's so obvious. He's been looking at a thing from the wrong angle. Believed what he wanted to believe. Let himself be led by his assumptions. He's made every rookie mistake. Now his fingers grasp the handle of the cart while she chews slowly. But Sandy isn't thinking about chocolate. Sandy's thinking about Max – about the hand that rested on Ollie's shoulder, like family. The hand that Ollie let slip from his sightline.

And here is Sandy, holding the rabbit in the air between them, giving him a hopeful smile, as if he still might believe her. It's too late, of course. The jig is up. Ollie is an empty pile of clothes, and Sandy hasn't breathed in ages.

THE BEAR

The first time Sandy saw the bear, in her panic she let him inside. She and Ollie were in a cabin at the Rushing River, about to go for a walk in the woods. Standing by the cabin door, hand on the door-knob, Sandy was queerily reminded of a horror film. "If this were a movie," she said, "we'd get picked off one by one." She looked at Ollie and wondered which of them would be the first to die. Then she turned the knob and opened the door a crack. A brown flash darted by her peripheral vision. Instead of slamming the door shut, she jerked it open. The big bear lumbered into the cabin. He was low, lurking, dangerous. He smelled the corners of the room, poked his nose under the cushions of the couch. Fear shot through Sandy's limbs, making them floppy and useless. But something was off; the bear was not a real bear, she realized. Perhaps it was a costume. "Is there a person in there?" Sandy asked the room, which was empty now, save her and the bear. "No," said the room.

The second time Sandy saw the bear she was standing with Ollie on the stairs off the cabin's back deck. A great brown bear came around the corner and climbed up the stairs and past her. He wore a striped tee shirt, like he was in the circus. The bear stopped and sniffed at Ollie. Terrified, Ollie slowly raised his arms in a this-is-a-stick-up pose. The bear mimicked him, raising up his paws.

Then Ollie curled over into a protective huddle and the bear ran his gums along the back of Ollie's neck.

We should probably talk about this, thought Sandy.

The third time, Sandy was prepared. She and Ollie went into the country store down the road and Sandy filled her basket with produce: giant zucchinis, grapes, acorn squash. She glanced at the cashier and then walked outside without paying. She was hungry, and she didn't know what she wanted. Surely her crime would be forgiven. Inside, the store began to flood with water. The water rose up, knocking shoppers off their feet. Ollie was thrown off balance, washed out of his clothes, as he splashed and somersaulted in the aisle. He floated out into the river that rushed behind them. Two policemen on shore waded into the river and took him by the arms. Sandy watched him from the bushes as they led him, naked, from the water to the muddy riverbank. Ollie lowered his eyes as they marched him forward, their hands gripped tight into his armpits.

Our little secret, Sandy thought. Brown fur flickered through the leaves across the river on the other side. She and the beast locked eyes. Sandy nodded to the bear.

Part Three

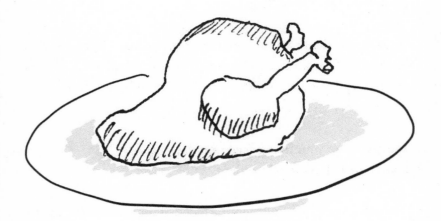

Your Feedback Is Important

Re-Birthing a New You Conference: Exit Survey
Name (optional): Spirit Rosenblatt
Please rate the following (space is provided for additional comments if desired):

Your overall experience at the Conference:
Poor/Fair/OK/Good/Excellent

First of all, thank you for allowing me to participate in this workshop. Thank you to Helen and Noah and all the generous facilitators. I had an excellent time. I don't understand the difference between "fair" and "ok."

The quality of your living accommodations:
Poor/Fair/OK/Good/Excellent

I stayed at the Playa Suites in the block of rooms set aside by the conference. It was good to have the camaraderie of the other participants. The room was clean. At times more privacy would have been helpful.

Which was your favorite seminar workshop, and why?

I found the "Tell Me What You Want" workshop most helpful. My partner was Grady from Alabama. We faced each other and repeated the question over and over. He said, "Tell me what you want." And I said, "To be a world-class, recognized life coach." He said, "Tell me what you want." I said, "To write guest columns in life coaching magazines." He said, "Tell me what you want." I said, "To help people realize their dreams." I recommend shortening this exercise because it is hard to face a stranger and answer this question repeatedly for an hour.

Interactions with the other participants:
Poor/Fair/OK/Good/Excellent

Well, the people were of course very nice. We are all here to grow and that was an exhilarating thing for me to be around. It has been my dream for so long to come here and be a part of this community, so it meant everything to me to finally meet everyone. When I first walked in the lobby and saw everyone drinking and talking and laughing it was nearly overwhelming. I have to give myself compassion because the body needs time to adjust and you can't just slide from one universe to another without some turbulence. As you know, I became quite ill. It may have been the shock to my system and it may have been a reaction to the alcohol, but I don't remember anything that happened that first day after my arrival, which I spent mostly in my bed with fever and chills.

When I walked into the conference hall the next morning everyone seemed bonded from all the team-building exercises they had done while I was sleeping. They had their own little groups. During the break I saw them playing ping-pong outside. They were screaming with laughter, and it was only ping-pong! You can't walk up to a table of people screaming like that and just join in. So I went across the street to Starbucks and couldn't decide what to order, and finally settled on a macchiato, but the barista who made it wore a nametag that said TRAINEE and she forgot to add the foam. I saw Grady and he remembered me from the reception and he said, "Hey, girlfriend!" and I started to cry. He was very kind about it. He sat with me outside while I drank my macchiato. Then we sat together at the "Tell Me What You Want" workshop. I felt very connected to Grady after that. Everyone had sectioned off at that point and now I had my little group and every one else had theirs and that was the way it was going to be and that was fine, that worked out very well.

What have you learned at the workshop that you did not anticipate learning?

Well, that Grady was attracted to me. I don't know why I didn't see it. I had talked to him like he was a girlfriend, baring every confidence and whatnot. We even held hands when we were outside one night and I thought that it was charming, because I have often wished that I had more male friends that I could do that with. I invited him into my room to eat the candy I had left in the mini-bar. We sat on my bed eating bite-sized Snickers and drinking Jim Beam from mini-bottles and giggling and Grady put his hand on my thigh. I thought, "Humans are so interesting. My leg is like a table to this man. Sometimes, a woman's leg is like a credenza."

Did the syllabus accurately reflect the workshop materials?

Grady and I spent the first several days together, and it was a comfort to have an ally in such an unfamiliar environment. He took to
calling me Chippy, as I was always chipper, and he would give me
a little poke in the ribs when he said it. I called him Ecks, or Eckie,
though neither of us could remember how come. After we did the
"Safe Falling" exercise with Karina and Daryl, we started hanging
out with them as well. Karina and Daryl knew each other from
last year's conference in New York. I regret to say that they would
encourage us to leave the seminar to go out drinking, which I did
not do but Grady did twice. It was good for me to have the empty
seat beside me when he wasn't there, because I focused more on
what the instructors were saying. I was concerned for Grady but
part of my task here is to understand where my boundaries end
and another person's begin. The lessons that are the most powerful
are often the most painful to learn. And not every learning comes
from the syllabus.

Mirror Communication
Poor/Fair/OK/Good/Excellent

At the Mirror Communication Workshop, we partnered with col-
leagues and shared our personal formation stories, mirroring each
other's gestures and mannerisms. My partner was Karina. She told
me about the time her grandmother from Poland passed away.
I told her the story of when I wet my pants during Brownies and
had to wash my underwear in the classroom sink.

I listened to Karina's story about her grandmother's death in a focused and gentle way. But when it was my turn, I did not feel that Karina was equally nurturing. As soon as I began, I must have made some gesture with my hands because Karina mirrored me and folded up her hands by her cheeks and said, "When you do that, you look like a puppy dog." She kept doing it every time I tried to make a point. She raised her hands like little paws, and said, "Oh, *I love it*." She started sticking her tongue out and panting. She shared this afterwards in the group reflection and then it became kind of a thing, a way to greet me.

Mirror communication is a powerful tool to use with clients to explore their dreams in a caring environment. But you must take care to pair people with partners who are ready to go to that safe space.

Did you take part in the "Letting Go of Resentment" seminar? If so, in what ways did you value the experience?

I took part in the Resentment workshop. Helen had us make a list of everyone we were angry at. I wrote down Tara Galbanni, who told everyone I wet my pants in Brownies. I wrote down my neighbor, Kimberly, who calls the dog catcher when my dog is off-leash. I wrote down Fergus, who cheated on me, and not just one time. I listed Karina and Daryl, and Grady, though only in my mind.

Helen said to make a new list and write down anybody on it we were not yet ready to forgive. I wrote down the same names. Helen just smiled and said, "You can call this list, 'Where You Can Find My Power.'"

Okay. I get that. I do.

Did you participate in the Closing Maypole? What Appreciations were reflected back to you?

I participated in the Closing Maypole Event. I had never braided a Maypole before but when the whistle blew, I ran across to the other side of the pole with my streamer while everyone else did the same. We had to call out one thing we appreciated about the person we were running past. Since I did not know people well enough to say what I appreciated, I just smiled at them. I was opposite Daryl, who wagged his tongue and called out, "Hi Weewee," which was what Chippy had morphed into, I guess from what I said about Brownies, and from the opening reception I don't remember, at which they say I did a lot of weeping.

What would you like the organizers to know so that we might improve on the conference for future participants?

Well, you should know that Grady is sleeping with Karina. I guess I should have seen it coming. But how can you prepare for that? How can you aspire for the best in people and let your mind believe that they will do the worst? I can't live like that. That night in my hotel room when I took off my shirt, Grady told me, "I'm going to remember the smile on your face right now for the rest of my life." And last night I heard him running in the hallway with Karina and she was squealing, like he pinched her. Why would he be pinching her? Do they want me to hear them? These are questions they will have to answer for themselves.

Is there anything you would like us to know that was not addressed in this evaluation form?

This morning I went back to Starbucks to get a macchiato and the same girl was working, the one in training. The AC was broken and the place was hot and stuffy. Grady and Karina were behind me, whispering, and the line was out the door. The customer at the register had a gift card that wouldn't scan and it took forever. The girl dropped the card twice and had to call her manager. There wasn't enough air for all of us to breathe.

When I got to the front of the line, the girl's face was red and she was miserable. She asked me, "Do you know what you want?"

Finally, the answer hit me. "I want you to forgive yourself," I said. She just stared. "Can you do that for me?"

She just stared at me. Then she said Yes. Yes, she could.

Can you believe it? She said *yes*. She smiled, and looked me straight in the eye.

FIVE KINDS OF DISASTER

1.   Act of God, 1997

Midge Pippick stares slack-jawed at the kumquats at Alpha Beta.
Bitter little oranges. What could you make with kumquats? Jello
salad. Fruitcake. She would look it up. A nice change. Twelve
minutes away, Max Pippick sits slack-jawed in the TV room,
a glassed-in patio lined with fraying rugs and rock-in-cement
Flintstones-style walls. He has stumbled on an unimaginable
world: *Barbarella.* The word rolls over in his mouth. *Barbarella.* On
TV, writhing, with no shirt on! He reaches in his pants for the very
first time. Works his way around. The room is spinning. *Barbarella.*
Barbarella… Barb – and then it's over. Blinded, reeling, he stumbles
towards the bathroom, pants around his knees. In his shellshock,
he walks straight through the sliding glass door, which is where,
kumquats in hand, his mother finds him.

2.   Levee Failure, 2004

Dusky-footed Woodrat Trail. Daylene on a hike with Skip Barnes.
Barnes likes to hike. Daylene does too. Or she could learn to. This

is her year to try new things. She made a picnic basket for their lunch: gouda cheese, sliced baguette, red grapes, which she popped into her mouth as she got dressed. Grape, grape, grape. Barnes had gone to Princeton, Daylene noted, as she draped mascara on her lashes and popped another grape. I hope he's smart. Not too smart. But smart. Just not too smart. *I can do this. Stretch your comfort zone, Dayle.* Grape, grape, grape. Doorbell ring. A sweaty handshake; is she shaking? Just some nerves. Deep up the trailhead forty minutes later, heading to the hills, Skip Barnes three paces behind Daylene on the narrow trail. Her whole face clammy now, grape grape grape. The rumbling begins.

3.   Tsunami, 2014

Spirit had a setback. She suffered a blow. She had a string of personal misfortunes. There was the toner cartridge, shaken when the plastic tab was already off, her cream silk blouse, her boss's contact lens. That was a mishap. There was the oil running low, so she checked it, and she added it, but she left the oil tank cap off, and the smoke wafted up but there was no stopping on the bridge, and she didn't know why they said that but she figured it was so you would not get hit. She read about a guy who pulled over on the bridge when he got rear-ended and the accident didn't kill him but another car hit his car and his car rolled forward and hit him and that threw him over the railing and he fell into the ocean. So she knew better than to stop. There was the callus remover blade she bought off of QVC that was a Smart Razor, that said it shaved away only callused skin; it was so smart it knew to stop at soft skin; it wouldn't cut it. That was an unfortunate accident. There was the blind date that was going so well, a new leaf, a light at the end of the tunnel, so well that she excused herself from her clam linguini and went into the restroom to put in her diaphragm right then and there, no awkward pauses later. She popped the case and lubed the rubber cup's soft rim. She put one foot on the toilet and pinched the bendy sides together; saw it sproing out of her hand and hit the wall, roll across the tiles and slip beneath the gap under the door into the restaurant, onto the green and yellow carpet. That was a misadventure. That was a regret.

4. Amusement Park Accidents, 2016

Fergus was documenting abandoned American structures. Gutted cathedrals, bombed-out tenements, deserted strip malls. Today he scaled the fence of Henderson's Fairy Waterworld, pushed through the juniper brambles, and gazed upon the rusted roller coasters. He snapped a photo with his Nikon. He could almost hear the music playing, smell the cotton candy. He had seen a documentary about a kind of people – not just one or two, but a whole subculture – who fell in love with objects, real romantic love, and they would want to fuck them, the buildings or vehicles or whatnot. One man loved a roller coaster. He would visit it like it was incarcerated, and he would soothe it, and talk to it, and rub himself against it. Whatever happened to that guy, he wondered. That kind of love is not sustainable. He took photos of the Tilt-a-Whirl, the light hitting it just so perfectly, sparking off it, showing new life and decay in the same instant. Unlit neon signs stood dully over ball tosses and water gun arcades. The party's over, he thought, *click click*. Abandoned Americana. That's what Americans do: they dream, they build, and then they throw it all away. Leave it for the landfill. He was British, so he had some perspective. For no good reason at all, water from the Mumblewark River trickled in through a pipe to the moat around the waterslide, an oasis that had never dried out. Oddly – and one could not expect this – there was a thriving alligator colony at this abandoned fairyland. Fergus weaved his way down the hot asphalt, camera pressed against his eye, taking in every lost, forgotten, useless, dazzling wonder.

5.   **Hostage Situation, 2017**

Alice drove while her boss's wife looked for house numbers. Usually Alice hostessed at Giuseppe's, but tonight a driver called in sick so there was no one to deliver pizzas. The boss's wife didn't like to drive at night and Giuseppe didn't trust Alice to take his car by herself. "I'll drive and you navigate," Alice had offered. So the two of them left together, each with a stack of warm square boxes.

This was not the first time Alice had been alone with the wife. Emiline was small, frail, nervous. Alice saw the way she moved around her husband. He never said a cross word to her, but Alice knew what she saw.

Tonight she tried again. "Anyone can get into a situation they don't know how to get out of," she said carefully as they drove down the tree-lined street. Emiline didn't speak. She never spoke when Alice tried to talk to her like this. She would look down and nod and hustle away. Alice kept trying to get through.

Now Emiline gazed out her window at the houses, their curtains drawn or windows tinged in warm yellows. "Left here," she said. Alice turned.

"Look, what I'm saying is," Alice went on, "all that means is that anyone can get out."

"Here," Emiline said.

Alice picked up the delivery sheet. "Which pizza?"

"This is my house," Emiline said. She opened her car door a crack. "I have a bag packed inside." She faced Alice – fifteen years her junior, combat-booted, tattooed birds on her wrists. "If you want to come with me," she said, "we can go to your house next."

Alice's heart careened in her chest. So she had been listening. "Then go where?" Alice asked.

Emiline smiled, not a broad smile, but a warm one. "You're the driver," she said. She got out, walked briskly to the front door and disappeared inside.

Alice waited. Her hands still grasped the steering wheel. The night air was perfect. She took a deep breath and slowly exhaled.

She turned to see if Emiline had come out yet. She had not. There was nothing there to see. Just a normal suburban house, trimmed and clean and still and dark and quiet.

MIGRATION

Abby suggested a hike. "We're in a rut," she said. "And I don't want to eat another piece of meat in a dark restaurant with you. You come see how *I* live for a change."

She did this to Robert periodically: presented him with some simmering frustration, some deep-seated failing of his that she'd probably been talking to her therapist and her mother, Betty, about for years. When she was in college, she'd sent him back a birthday check he had mailed her. The note said, "Thank you for the money. Now please go into a store – any store – and think of me. Imagine what I might want as a gift. Please send that back to me instead." He sent her a bird feeder. She mailed him a heartfelt note after that one and moved that battered perch from apartment to apartment. The truth is, the only reason he sent her the birdfeeder is because he ordered one for himself and the company had accidentally sent him two. At least he'd had the good sense to shut up about that.

Now, it seemed, he was guilty of taking his daughter out to too many dark restaurants that served too much meat. Which revealed a disinterest and unwillingness to get to know her in her own life. He *did* know Abby – that was what she'd never understand. He knew her better than she knew herself. He knew how she'd fought against the bottle when he'd tried to feed her, so hungry and angry and not understanding that all she needed to do was relent. She never let anything go. *Walk away from suffering*, he wanted to tell her. *Sometimes there's nothing there to fight.*

So here they were, looping around Lake Anza. He was just back from Spain, writing about the bullfighters in Pamplona. Soon he would be packing for his next gig in Istanbul. But for now he walked behind his daughter, who wore bright blue sport shoes and carried a body-hugging thermos made of thick red fabric strapped to her hip. Her ponytail bobbed out the back of her baseball cap and she talked to him as he followed her on the trail. He couldn't hear much of what she was saying and got lost in the cadence of her voice. It was like a song, and it mixed in with the wind through the oak trees and the music from the sparkling creek they crossed on a mossy wooden footbridge. He breathed in the sweet afternoon air.

"Have I stunned you into silence?" Abby asked. She was looking over her shoulder. Her face was pink and coated in a light sheen of perspiration.

Robert smiled back at her. "No. I'm just enjoying the view. You're right. This is better than a steak. Though I'm not swearing off steak forever," he added. "Just for one day."

Abby's expression didn't change in an obvious way, yet it turned sour. It sank inward and then rose forth again, hard and knowing. Robert tried to calculate what was happening.

She turned her head and kept walking. Robert followed in her wake. Her gait was stiffer now.

"I'm sorry," he said. "It's hard to hear you. I missed the last thing you said."

Abby soldiered on. "It doesn't matter."

"I'm listening now. Tell me what you said."

"What was the last thing you heard?" she challenged.

She had been talking about work. About visiting her friend Jessie in Portland. He didn't know. She'd said the words "nocturnal" at one point and "so pedestrian," and Robert was struck by their lyricism, by the beauty of words as they flowed from his daughter's mouth. But that was minutes ago. Hours?

"I don't know. Let's not make a game of chicken out of this, Abby. Tell me what you wanted me to hear."

"A game of chicken?" she asked, stopping and turning around. "I'm sorry. How is this a game?"

The trees circled all around him as he balanced in his hard-soled shoes. "It's not a game," Robert said.

She waited him out for a moment and then started walking again.

Abby spoke quietly. "I don't want you to go on your trip." The cut of the air made her words land in Robert's ear somehow, as if they were talking into tin cans on a string. She sounded like a little girl.

"Why not?"

"I don't have a good feeling," she said. "I can't explain it."

"I'm not going anywhere dangerous. This is a nothing trip. This is a little vacation."

Her ponytail bobbed with her steps. Robert waited but no more came. "What's this about?"

"I don't like it when you travel. I just don't feel good about it this time."

He knew he should comfort her, but he couldn't help but feel pleased with this development. After so many years of being in the doghouse with her at every turn, her fretfulness was an unexpected glory.

"Nothing bad is going to happen to me, honey," Robert offered. "Nothing ever has, and nothing ever will."

"That's provably false."

Provably false. When had she gotten this vocabulary?

"I'll tell you exactly how I'm going to die," he told her. "Abby, stop."

She stood above him on the trail, her nostrils flaring like a baby bull.

"I will be ninety-five years old. I will go to Sears to buy a pair of track pants and I will have a heart attack in the parking lot. I will die in peace, of old age." He should have stopped there, but he didn't. He never knew when to stop. "And no one will remember me."

Her face crumpled. She turned around. "Fuck you, Dad," the little voice said. His stomach went queasy. He had as good intentions as anybody. Why did he always cap out at being an asshole?

"That's not a bad thing, Abby. Nothing lasts forever. Twenty people will read my books. But you'll remember me."

Just then a hiker rounded the path behind her with a drooling, panting Rottweiler in the lead.

"Afternoon," said a man Robert's age, wearing what looked like Spandex cycling shorts. The dog jostled around Abby.

"Afternoon," Robert said to the man. He said it firmly, a little too loudly, a little old-boy friendly. Really the man's shorts made Robert want to laugh, made him want to push him down the cliff. The Rottweiler tumbled into Robert's crotch, sniffing it with abandon.

"*No!*" Robert snapped.

Then the dog was gone, the hiker was gone, as quickly as they had been there. A slimy track of drool across Robert's groin was all that remained. "Great," he said. He tried to wipe it off. When he looked up, his daughter had walked ahead and was nowhere in sight.

"Abby," he called, hustling to catch up. "I'm sorry." But he knew that he was right. Maybe once he had been destined for greatness, had lived his life as if shot from a cannon. Not anymore. *They won't tell stories about me when I'm gone*, he thought, *but you'll remember me.*

"Abby, wait," he called again. "Come on."

There she was. Robert caught a glimpse of her bright blue heel as it flashed up ahead. Then she turned a corner, and he couldn't see her anymore.

WHAT'S LEFT AT THE END

Jessie is waiting for me at the Portland airport, waving and calling my name. She wears baggy white shorts, a blue tank top and flip-flops. Large and small black circles drawn with a thick felt pen dot her thighs like a chalkboard strategy diagram at a football game.

I reach out to hug her and mean to say, "Hi, Sweetie," but when the words come out of my mouth they are different. They say, "What the hell?"

"Hey, Zing," she says. "I don't want to talk about it. I'll tell you in the car." She looks up at the baggage claim sign. "Do you have a bag?"

I do, and we wait for it at the carousel. I scan each passing suitcase for my own but they all look like mine, so instead I watch the other waiting passengers, certain one of them will steal my bag and I'll be stuck in these sweatpants for a week. Everyone is looking back at me. Then I realize they are staring at Jess's legs.

In the car ride toward downtown Portland, she explains. It's for the radiation tomorrow. She has come straight from the hospital and the technician has marked on her legs all the places they will zap her with their lasers. "I thought you were just going in for follow-up tests," I say. My voice a bright noise, a squeak.

"They found some tumors in my bones and want to get those now, too," she says. "But they could have told me they were going to draw on me. I would have worn long pants. Stupid fuckers."

Her cursing unnerves me: this from a woman who never curses. This from a woman I have actually heard use the word "cockadoody" as an expletive.

"Nobody looks at legs anyway," I say. "People look at faces. There have been studies."

She turns and gives me a look. She is feigning annoyance, and it gives me some relief. I have broken her bad mood.

"Men look at faces, then boobs, then hands," I say. "Women look at teeth and then hair. They never look at legs."

Now she is laughing a little.

"In fact," I say, "I'm naked from the waist down right now. And tell me you didn't notice."

I come downstairs later for dinner and she is lying on the couch, stretched out like a rag doll with her arm dangling over the side. Her mouth is open and her eyes are closed.

Her cat, Snacks, a fat tortoiseshell, is perched above her head, eyeing me and flicking his fluffy tail.

The stair creaks and she opens her eyes and sits up. She wipes her chin with the back of her hand.

"Oh my God, was I drooling?" she says. "I'm so wiped out."

"Let me make you some dinner," I say.

"You?"

"Yes, me," I say indignantly. "I was thinking I would make you Chinese food in those little white boxes."

"My favorite," she says. "There are menus on top of the fridge."

I come back with them and we circle chicken wrapped in lettuce leaf, egg foo yung and pot stickers. "Your hands are shaking," she tells me.

"I must be hungry," I say. "My hands shake when I get low blood sugar." This is true. But I don't have low blood sugar now.

Ezra calls from Newark while we're waiting for the food to arrive. He was already away on a business trip when the hospital scheduled the dates for Jess's tests. She told him not to come back. I would be here first, and her parents were coming from Laconia on Wednesday. There would be plenty of people here to keep her company, she told him. I pick at a hangnail while she takes his call.

Later, we sit on the couch and eat off plates I gave them as a wedding present. Through the window, lights from the houseboats twinkle in the harbor below. "Tell me about Carlo," she says, trying gingerly to bring a chicken and lettuce wrap to her lips.

"He's okay," I say. "He's pretty good. I like him."

She waits a minute and then raises her eyebrows for more. "That's it?" she says. "What is he like? What does he do for fun?"

"Um, right now he's building a robot with his friend Breck. When they're done they're going to enter it into contests where it fights with other robots until one of them dies."

She spits out some bean sprout when she laughs at this. "That's good, Abby," she says. "He sounds creative and ambitious. Those are important qualities in a mate." She picks the bean sprout off the coffee table and eats it.

"Is it serious?" she asks.

"I don't know. I don't know if we're on the same track. There's another guy at my office I'm having a little flirtation with. Maybe he's the one I'm supposed to be with."

"You're good at keeping men in the hopper," she says. "Keeping your placeholders. You just lack follow-through."

I don't say anything for a moment and neither does she.

When I look up, her head is tilted to the side with a familiar expression of concern, and I don't like it. "Why do you give me that look sometimes, like I'm crying, when I'm not?" I say.

It comes out sharper than I expect it to. She pokes at a potsticker with her chopsticks. I work a cabbage strand that's stuck between my teeth until it comes out and I swallow it.

"What time do we have to get up tomorrow?" I ask.

"I have to be there at eight," she says. "But you can get there whenever you want."

"Of course I'll go there with you."

"You don't have to. You'll just be waiting around for me all morning."

"That's when I want to go," I say.

"Okay," she says.

"I'm sorry," I say.

"There's nothing to be sorry for," she answers, and I think about this statement for a long time that night before I fall asleep.

When I see her in the morning I remember my dream from the night before, of dark circles dancing up my arms, an army of blind ants. Jess wears long pants today, and I try not to stare at her legs.

She can't eat breakfast but asks me to pick up turkey sandwiches on twelve-grain bread, crisp apples and sour candy at the store while she is getting zapped. She'll stay in the hospital tonight. I drop her off and watch her walk through the sliding front doors, and then drive to one deli, a produce market, a supermarket and three corner stores trying to fulfill my mission. When I meet her at eleven, she looks visibly relaxed in her hospital gown and bathrobe, and the black circles on her legs are gone.

We go out onto the patio off the fourth floor to eat lunch. I bite into my apple – it's soft and grainy – and lean back on the bench and squint at the sun. It's nice up here. They have lined the patio with ficus trees and spidery ferns in giant planters. I catch myself thinking that when this is over, when Jess is dead, I should come back here with a book and sit in the sun and read. As if I have found a new park, a new spot to hang out in Portland.

She brushes my cheek with her thumb.

"What?" I say.

"Nothing," she says. "Just some schmutz."

I wipe my face with my fingers.

"It's gone," she says.

"What was it?" I ask.

"It's nothing," she says. "It's gone."

The sliding glass doors shush open across the patio, but when I look up, there's nobody there.

"I saw Yvette at Target before I left, did I tell you?" I say.

"Yvette from UNH?"

"She works at Charles Schwab now. She says she's a 'Change Manager.'"

"What does that mean?" Jess asks. She bites mushily into her apple.

"That's what I asked." I take on Yvette's too-bright demeanor and say, "She said, 'It means exactly what it sounds like. I *manage change.*'"

"But what does it *mean?*" says Jess, laughing.

"It *means…*" I say, still using Yvette's now squeakily defiant voice, "… It *means* I *manage change!*" By now we are both laughing, hard. And then I take a bad turn. I feel my chest tighten and convulse with a laughter I can't stop.

Finally, I slow down and wipe my eyes. "Hoo," I say.

After lunch, we gather up our things and head back inside.

We walk toward her room, passing a medical scale along the
way. I step on.

"How much do you think my clothes weigh?" I ask.

"I don't know," she says. "A lot. Ten pounds."

"Okay. Good."

I move the measures along their tracks. When I turn and look
at her she is standing with a slightly vacant look in her eyes, as if
waiting for a bus. I step off the scale.

We sit on her bed and play cards in the afternoon, flanked on
one side by a watercolor of a country lane with a horse leaning
over a fence, and on the other by a poster that says "Teamwork" in
cursive, as if stolen from some executive conference room.

As dinner time approaches we decide I'll rent a movie, when
Ezra calls on the hospital phone. Jess settles back into her pillows
and tells him what he is missing. She tells him about the radiation
technician this morning, an older Filipino gentleman who called
her "My baby." ("Now don't move, my baby. One more time and
then we are done, my baby.") About the vending machine that sells
diet cupcakes and the rasping cough we hear through the wall from
the room next door.

I feel intrusive, so I mouth, "Say hi for me" and walk through
the maze of hallways, spilling out into the night with a *shush* of the
sliding doors.

At the video store, I scan the shelves, seeking. Should it be "Big
Momma's House"? "The Sound of Music"? Something uplift-
ing. I look in the comedy section. "Deuce Bigelow: Male Gigolo."
Nothing is right. I float down the aisles and imagine she is already
dead. "Jess is dead," I think, "and this is what it feels like." I try to
wear it like a coat. "Okay," I think. "Jess is dead and it's sad, it's

horrible, but I can tolerate it. I can wear this coat."

I choose "Cool Hand Luke" and "The Joy Luck Club" and bring them to the front. A bored-looking middle-aged woman sits on a stool by the register reading a paperback. Her gray hair is flat and dull in a ponytail. I hand her the movies and Jess's video membership card. She looks at the card and then at me.

"Are you Jessie Kitchell?" she asks.

"She's my friend. It's her account."

She punches some numbers in the computer. "I can't accept this card," she says. "Your name isn't on the account."

"She just told me to come pick up the movies. She authorized me to use her account," I say. "The movies are for her."

"Customers don't have the power to authorize others to use their account," she says, handing the card back to me. "This isn't valid for you. Do you have an account here?"

"No," I say. "I don't live here. Can you call her? She'll tell you that it's fine if I use the account."

"How would I know it's her?" she asks.

"Because she'll *tell you* it's her," I say, starting to crackle and spark. "Don't you have a password you can ask her or something?"

"Anyone can answer a telephone," she says.

"Look," I say, "She's going to be dead before this card expires. She can't come get the movies herself. That's not going to happen."

My temper does not move her. She picks up her dimestore novel. "You can yell at me all you want," she says, turning to her dog-eared page. "I can't let you check out these movies."

"Fine." My voice is a bark from somewhere in my chest. "Then take it!" I toss the DVD box at her and I mean for it to fly nowhere, but it leaves my hand and the corner hits her in the eye. She drops her book and covers her face with her hands.

"Why did you do that? Why did you do that?" she moans. She bends over herself weeping.

I stand there. A terror courses through me as she rocks in her seat. She looks up and her skin is bleeding and the eyelid is starting to swell. "Why did you do that to me?" she says. "I didn't do anything to you."

"I'm so sorry," I say. "It was an accident."

"Get out of here," she says bitterly, pressing her fingers against the blood.

"Do you want me to call the police?" I ask.

"Get out of here, you crazy bitch," she says. "Go to hell."

I realize I'm still holding the other movie in my hand so I put it on the counter. I walk out to the car and sit for a minute before I think maybe she really is calling the police, so I start the engine and drive back to the hospital.

I tell Jess I couldn't use her card and leave out all the rest. We end up sitting together on her bed and watching *Cagney and Lacey* on TV. It's as if we're in a time warp: the room, the art, and the TV all look as if they have come from the 1980s, and here we are watching Sharon Gless hotfooting it after a red Chrysler LeBaron. It's as if we never grew up at all.

"I remember the first time I met you," I say.

"So do I," she says. "At that barbecue off-campus. Whose barbecue was it?"

"I can't remember. I just remember being there and not knowing anyone, and you were there and you didn't know anyone, and we started talking in the back, by those stone steps."

"That's right," she says. "And you said you chose your class schedule based on which classes started after eleven a.m. I thought that was funny."

"And we talked about mis-heard song lyrics. You sang, '*Fly robin, fly. Fly robin, fly. Way up in the sky.*' Only you thought it was about a fly, robbing another fly. That's my first memory of you."

"Hm," she says. She pours some crushed ice from a paper cup into her mouth. "That's funny. I remember that party. But I never thought that. That must have been somebody else."

In the bathroom, I sit down on the toilet and I think about the black circles the doctors drew on Jess's legs. What is wrong with people?

When I come out, a nurse is in the room with a beige metal and plastic machine. It's a humidifier of some kind, and the nurse is explaining to Jess how to put her face in it when a timer goes off, to help clear out her lungs. It has a rectangular tunnel at the top, with a soft rubber runner around the opening. The nurse sets a few dials, closes the panel at the opening, and leaves. The machine lets out a heavy sigh and begins to whir.

"Why do all the machines in this place sound like they're breathing?" I ask. It's the wrong question, I realize too late. The machines are breathing because the people aren't.

Jess walks to the window and slides slippers onto her feet. I have never asked her for a prognosis. I think I've done this to protect her, to save her from having to repeat bad news. But I realize now that I have been protecting me.

"So what are the next steps?" I say.

Assuming the tests come out okay, for now she's done. *Done.* Then she comes in every three months and they check her to see if anything new is there.

"Every three months?" I ask. "Even though they said this was so aggressive?"

"Yes," she shrugs. "I guess they can't see it until it's this big," she says, making a circle with her finger and thumb. "But that's already millions of cells."

"So you just go in and they check you and say, 'Oh, it's gotten smaller, it's gone away?'"

"Well, with this kind of cancer," she says, walking back toward me, "they tell you if something new is there, not really if something has gone away." She looks at me and her green eyes are a little bloodshot.

The timer on the humidifier dings like an Easy-Bake Oven and Jess slides open the plastic door. White steam pours out, rushes up and engulfs us. For a moment, we are lost in the fog, blind to each other, the room, the machines, and everything else that has happened.

"Hey, Jessie," I say. "Look, we're in heaven."

I can almost make out her face in the mist in front of me.

DINOSAURIA

Robert Zinger was sixty-four years old and he felt it. He knew it in his bones, which creaked, and his skin, which bled more easily now when scratched; he knew it in his teeth, worn down from gnashing in his sleep, and yellow, with one brown one in the back. He knew it in his eyes, which tired when he read the paper in the evenings and which became dry in colder temperatures. But in his hair, Robert had not aged a day since grade school. His hair was soft and silky, its color straw blond, its texture fine, and no matter how he cut it, it hung impishly from his brow, dancing teasingly above his left eye. And it was because of his boyish hair that here, in the dim light of the bar, he knew that the woman had mistaken him for someone else. A younger version of himself – perhaps the Robert of the 1970s, when he had trod up Market Street with his compadres in arms, protesting the Vietnam War. Perhaps she mistook him for his later self, the man he was in the '80s, an aspiring novelist who banged out sentimental angst on his Smith Corona, trying to carve a place among the icons he tried inconspicuously to emulate, before despairing at his failure and falling into budget travel writing in the '90s. Then he forgot his despair altogether, except sometimes, when it would hit him in a curious pang, a confusing prick, like the time he ran after a bus that would not wait for him when he was sure the driver heard his cries, and he was so angry that he chased it for a block until he had to stop, bent over and gasping for his breath, as a sudden and piteous self-degradation overwhelmed him and he found himself shielding back tears.

Tonight the woman was smiling at him, leaning close and shouting with sweet breath in his ear over the music, placing her hand on his shoulder as if only to steady herself as their faces came alongside each other. Her name was Spirit, and though he had not known this before tonight he had seen her before, was well aware of Spirit, and the way her own shoulders were smooth and pale beneath the tank tops she wore as she walked their neighborhood every afternoon with her dog, a wiry, snaggle-toothed boxer she called Niffy. The dog had smelled Robert's own feet more than once as he stopped and pretended to greet it, petting it and looking into its milky eyes as it drooled and choked excitedly for air through its face, compressed as if it had run into a wall. He would steal glimpses at Spirit's legs, brown hairs peeking illicitly where she stopped shaving above her sturdy calves, and stare wantonly at the freckles on her knees.

Now the dog lay at their feet at the bar. Robert could see its barrel torso rise and fall quickly in sleep, an occasional paw softly pushing at his ankle as it twitched in a dream. He had never seen Spirit without the dog, in fact. She trailed behind it on a long retractable leash, as if the dog were walking her, and she following it with an energetic bounce in her step as the dog zigged and zagged, peeing gratuitously as Spirit cooed praise. Robert nodded to her once as he passed and she had beamed back at him and said nonsensically, "I'm walking my dog!"

He had slid onto the barstool tonight next to Spirit as she was sipping a pink Cosmopolitan and shouting conversation to the bartender, a bearded man in a leather vest who looked up at Spirit and nodded periodically while he shook drinks, rang up customers, and sometimes left the area altogether. Spirit kept smiling, undeterred, and when the bartender would return, her shouted pleasantries would continue. The bar was one of the newer ones since gentrification had overwhelmed downtown and his old haunts had disappeared, one by one.

She sat quietly for a minute next to Robert and twirled a plastic sword in her drink while Robert pretended to check messages on his phone. Then she turned her body to him and spoke into his ear.

"I'm celebrating tonight," she said. He could smell the grapefruit on her tongue.

"What are you celebrating?" he leaned in and called back to her. Her brown hair fluttered behind her ear.

"I got my CPPC degree," she said. She held up her bar glass, which sparkled and quivered in her hand. "I'm a Certified Personal and Professional Coach."

"Congratulations," he said, and as he clinked her glass he added, "Chin chin."

"Chin chin," Spirit said. She pressed the rim against her lips and drank. She swirled the liquid around in the glass and watched it eddy.

Spirit turned to her reflection in the mirror across the bar. Robert watched her in the mirror, too. Her hair, pinned back in two barrettes, was flat and tired from a day at the office, and her cream silk blouse showed a smudge that looked like ink just below the collar. She wore bracelets on both wrists, the kind his daughter used to call bangles – ten or twenty thin metal loops that, aside from their bright colors, looked vaguely militaristic.

Robert's daughter, Abby, hadn't worn bangles for years. She'd told him, when she was in her early twenties and dating a Republican, that a woman should always wear seven accessories, no more, no less. "Any less and you look underdressed; any more and you look trashy," she said. She pointed to each one on her body as she reeled off the list: ring, ring, watch, necklace, earrings, belt, barrette. The Republican boyfriend hadn't lasted, much to Robert's relief, but the little girl with the jangling array of noise on her wrists seemed to be gone forever. Her mother, Betty, was gone as well – a woman who used to drive a battered yellow Volvo and decorate their garden with statues she'd made out of clay, who once scrawled "YES" in drying cement while they strolled Abby and her baby brother Ollie along the sidewalk one bright afternoon. These days he didn't know what kind of car Betty drove, and she hadn't missed Robert for years.

Robert tried to count Spirit's accessories. Barrette, barrette, some kind of shiny pin on her lapel, a necklace with what looked like red and blue wooden beads, and those bangles, which took her way above the limit. Yet Robert would not say that Spirit looked trashy. Far from it.

"What sport do you coach?" Robert asked, as he downed the last bit of his whiskey and gestured for another. He wadded up his damp napkin into a ball.

Spirit turned and looked at him guardedly.

Robert saw by the tilt of her head and droop in her smile that he had hurt her feelings. His head felt light with panic. A car honked loudly in the intersection outside the bar and one man cursed at another before tires screeched away. "You said you got your coaching license. What sport?" Spirit continued to stare.

"It's not that kind of coaching," she said. "I'm a personal and professional coach. I help people listen to their dreams and discover their true passion. I coach them to regain the '*they*' that is their birthright. Not the *they* that they *are*, but the *they* that they *be*."

His mind stuttered as he tried to make sense of it. His thoughts cycled in a static loop.

"For example," she went on, "who are you?" She asked him plainly.

"I'm Robert Zinger," he said. It came out sounding like an alibi.

"That's who you are," Spirit said. "Now tell me who you *be*."

Robert let the grammatical absurdity of her question wash over him. He thought of Spirit's hardy calves, the relentless optimism of her gait as she bounded through the neighborhood after her slathering dog, and just then his desire for her nearly overwhelmed him. He looked away and brought his drink to his lips with a shaky hand.

"I know you from the neighborhood," he said. "I see you walking your dog."

"I've seen you, too," Spirit answered.

"I've never seen you without that dog," he said, looking down at the flaking beast.

"The love of my life," she said. "My little squirrel chaser." She rubbed her foot along the dog's bristled back. "Dogs have a lot that they can teach people, you know," she said. "They love you even when you're not your best self. Their capacity for forgiveness is awesome."

Women and their dogs, Robert thought. Still, she had seen him in the neighborhood. That surprised him. He had thought himself to be invisible to women for quite a while.

"I'm just Robert Zinger," he told her. He tossed his wadded up napkin over the bar, where it landed on the ground next to a plastic bin. "Budget travel writer. I yam what I yam. I be what I be."

"That's what most people think," Spirit said. She sipped the

last of her Cosmopolitan and Robert waved to the bartender for
another. "They don't know their true capacities. Like my mother,"
she went on. "I went to visit her and my stepdad, Gebhardt, one
day with Niffy. While I was over, my mom went into the basement
and I didn't see her go downstairs. I noticed the basement door was
open and the light was on, so I turned it off and locked the door.
I didn't want Niffy to go down there."

"Oops," said Robert.

"Oops. Human error," Spirit answered. "She was enraged with
me. *Enraged.* She was down there in the cold and dark, and it
frightened her. But instead of dealing with her fear, she channeled
it as anger, and anger needs a victim."

Robert had a vision of Betty then, channeling her anger. He
couldn't remember his particular failing on that day, but could see
her face so clearly, her eyes hard, her shoulders turned away.

"Sorry your mom got mad at you," Robert told her.

"It's just the way she moves in the world," said Spirit. "She does
the best she can."

Robert pondered this. Maybe it was all one could ask for.

The two of them sat next to each other quietly for a long time,
with the hairs on their forearms touching and the music throbbing
against their ears and the drinks refilled by the bartender. At some
point Robert turned to her and said, "Can I walk you home?" and
they slid off their seats and he helped her put on her coat. When
Spirit stirred, the dog woke up and jostled around Robert's legs and
lumbered out the door in front of them. The air was crisp, the night
was clear, and Robert Zinger took Spirit's hand as they moved
underneath the moonlight. Car headlights shone in their faces and
then sped past.

"Don't tell my neighbors I'm letting her walk off-leash," Spirit said, as Niffy nosed an abandoned paperback book on the sidewalk and then urinated on it. "They report me."

"Your neighbors are douchebags," Robert said. Her hand was soft and warm, and he reached it up and kissed it. She smiled, her eyes dewy, and swung his hand in hers.

The dog lumbered on before them, leaving drops of drool on the pavement as it weaved, looking as drunk as the two of them. They walked by a house with a spindly apricot tree out front and Robert grabbed one of the hard fruits as they passed. He tossed it in the air twice and caught it with the same hand.

"Who do you be, Spirit?" Robert asked her.

Spirit turned and took a breath in and Robert saw something familiar in her then, a glimpse of expectation in her eyes. He couldn't remember the last time someone looked at him that way, or who it had been. He lobbed the apricot into the street, where it bounced and skittered, wriggled like a mouse.

A clabbering of toenails scratched the sidewalk then; Robert saw a flurry of movement in the corner of his eye as Niffy came alive, taut and muscular, an animal fixing on its prey. Spirit dropped his hand, brought her bangle-covered wrists up to her face, pulled at her cheeks and screamed, and Robert remembered who it was she triggered in his memory. It was Abby.

The dog shot into the street, eyes fixed on the apricot, as if the lights of the cars upon it were the stars shining down from a vast and limitless sky. An SUV hit it with a disastrous thud. It sounded like a person, Robert thought, the weight of it, a breath expelled like a child's frustrated sigh.

They were all in the street then, Robert kneeling on the pavement as Spirit sobbed and wailed over her dog, its eyes unfocused in confusion and its breathing a wet rattle. The driver of the SUV was on the phone, calling someone, and other cars in both directions stopped. Robert pictured them later at the emergency vet, waiting expectantly for the doctor to come out with news. He would sit with her for as long as it took to hear. He would comfort her, and maybe after it was done he would walk her to her home and she might forgive him. He would help her through the long, dark night if she would let him. Robert knew that in the morning Spirit would see him in the sunlight – see that he was old enough to be her father, old enough to be her uncle at the least. Any future was untenable. But then, any future had been untenable for some time now, so he was used to that.

CONCESSIONS

The movie is post-apocalyptic. A desolate army outpost sits in the shadow of a giant, rusted-out Ferris Wheel in a barren wasteland.

"No one would ride on that," my mother leans over and whispers in my ear. "It's a bulls-eye target for the enemy!"

"Shh," I tell her. "It's a fantasy."

"It still has to make sense," she says. She straightens her back against her seat, sniffs, then a minute later says, "I'm going to get some popcorn."

She stands up and sidles past the high school kids that line our row, then feels her way down the steps, waving her arm for a railing that isn't there. I lurch in my seat when she teeters, but she catches herself, and it doesn't matter because I couldn't have gotten there in time anyway. I finally exhale when the square of light washes in and then narrows to black as the theater door swings shut behind her.

Four scenes later, in a dilapidated, burned-out office building, war-grizzled men argue about who will pay for candy bars sold by a wandering refugee. Terrorists did blow up that Ferris Wheel; she was right. And I realize with a gnawing dread that she's been gone for way too long.

I push past the high school students and make my way down the stairs toward the exit, waving my arms in front of me in the darkness. Once in the lobby, I'm momentarily disoriented by the identical entrances to screen after screen in the multiplex, a dizzying carpet of geometrical patterns lining the path that runs between them. Then I see her, alone, standing at the concession counter. She stands so still I wonder at first if she has fallen asleep on her feet.

"Betty?" I say quietly. I press my hand flat against her back. Her lips are pursed and she is angry.

"There's nobody here!" she says. "There's no one in the whole place! It's a ghost town out here!" I look around. The lobby is abandoned.

"Have you been standing here the whole time?"

"I'm hungry," she says. I notice that her posture is stooped.

"What did you eat with Ollie?" I ask her. She spent the day with my brother going shopping.

"We didn't have time for lunch," she tells me, still looking around for the non-existent concession worker. "I wanted to watch the ice skating in the outdoor rink they put up next to Macy's and Ollie had to get some appliance for his computer."

"But you were gone all day." A familiar burn rises at my brother. Ollie once called our family "a trick that isn't going to work." He still comes by, but he just goes through the motions. How he manages to make things worse without leaving any trace still astounds me.

"Don't be such a fuss-budget, Abby," my mother says. "I'm capable of feeding myself." Little white balls of saliva gather at the corners of her mouth. She looks a hundred years old.

"I'll go find someone," I say. I march across the stained carpet, which seems to undulate beneath my feet. "Hello?!" I call out. I walk by giant dioramas of coming attractions. In one you can put your face in a cut-out window next to the movie stars. Another has a dog driving a car with a man cowering in the back seat. "Is anybody working here?"

I walk up an ornate staircase as wide as my living room, which opens in both directions in the middle. I take the left side and feel myself breathing hard when I get to the top. A teenage boy in a maroon uniform shirt pushes a carpet sweeper along the floor.

"There's no one at the concession stand downstairs," I say. He looks up at me blankly. "The movie is still on. Are you open downstairs, or what?"

"We're open," he says. "There should be people there."

"Well, there aren't," I say.

"Yeah," he says, thinking it over. "There should be people down there."

I'm wasting my time, I think. I go back downstairs to the concession, where a young woman is now behind the counter laughing it up with my mother. The smell of fresh popcorn warms the air, and the popping noise accelerates as white kernels overflow the canister and tumble onto the tray below.

"There was no one here," I say to the woman.

"I had to get more butter," she answers. She and my mother share a look and I have to bat away the flickering notion that they have been talking about me.

"You should have more people working here," I say. She ignores me and rearranges the popcorn to make room for more. "Get whatever you want," I say to my mother. "Do you want a hot dog? You should eat something."

"I'm getting popcorn," Mom says.

"That's not enough," I tell her.

She scowls at me. "I'm getting popcorn!"

There's nothing more I can do. I shake my head and wait while the girl scrapes the popcorn and scoops it into a red and white-striped sack the size of a small grocery bag. She hands my mother her popcorn. "Twelve dollars."

"I've got it," I say, reaching in my purse for my wallet. "Twelve dollars, Jesus." I open my wallet and pull out six singles – everything I have. "Do you have any money?" I say sheepishly. She pulls out a twenty dollar bill and pays with it.

"I can put it on my card," I say.

"Don't worry about it." She puts a fistful of popcorn in her mouth. "This movie is terrible," she says. "I'm ready to go home."

The theater is on the second level of an outdoor shopping mall. My mother and I walk outside and lean over the railing and watch people move down the cobbled pathway below like cars on an underpass. The mall is lit up with twinkling Christmas lights and the air is getting chill. Giant shining balls hang from the trees. Clusters of young people careen through families and couples, sometimes shrieking and chasing each other. From here it looks like they are dressed in costumes – some with their faces painted blue or green and some wearing what look like ball gowns. They are headed to the other end of the mall.

The row of restaurants on our level catches my eye and I realize that I'm starving. "Let's get a real bite to eat," I say.

We go to a cafe that serves only food on skewers. I am ravenous when the waitress puts our food on the table. "I hate this," my mother says. "*Gimmicky food.* Everything has to have a gimmick these days."

"It's good though, isn't it?"

"Oh, I'm not complaining."

She slides chicken and green peppers onto her plate. "How's

Henry liking his job?"

"It's okay," I answer. Henry is my boyfriend of two years. He has been working for our city councilwoman for one of them. "I guess he thought it would be better. He thought he wouldn't get bossed around so much." I picture Henry then, pushing away from the dining table, his whole body lately radiating with the word "long-suffering." It's a thankless job, and I wonder how long he will last.

"Some people don't like a woman with an opinion," my mother says. I look at her and don't know what to make of it. Does she mean he's with me because I don't have opinions? I can't get the question I want to ask her to form in my mouth.

"That's not it," I say. I turn to the menu on the wall behind the register to see if this place sells wine, but I can't read the menu from here. I need to get glasses.

"Look what happened with your brother and Sandy," Mom says.

"Sandy cheated on Ollie with his best friend," I say. "I think that was the dominant sticking point."

"That's what Ollie *said* was the sticking point," she says, sucking her diet soda from the straw. "Nobody knows what goes on inside a relationship."

God knows that's true, I think, remembering the heavy, silent years in my childhood home before my father moved out.

"Sandy married Max Pippick six months after she and Ollie broke up," I say. "Are we really debating this?"

"Eat," my mother says, pointing at my plate with her skewer. "You're hungry."

I put an oily chunk of grilled onion in my mouth. "You're the one who skipped lunch."

A group of teenage girls runs by us wearing their pajamas,

carrying big, bulky stuffed animals.

"What's going on down there, anyway?" I ask, peering down the walkway. The low thrum of a rock band's bass floats up toward us, punctuated by laughter.

"It's a holiday party, or early New Year's, or something," my mom says.

"They're in costume, though."

"We dressed in costume for holiday parties. We dressed up, anyway."

A man walks by us on stilts, in a hurry. We're finished with our dinner then, my mother and I. And as we have so often done, like two peas in a pod, two birds of a feather, two women born with the same small bladder – we set off to find a bathroom.

We stop before we get there to take a closer look at the revelers. They are not just high school students; there are people of all ages, dressed up in gowns and dark suits and pajamas and costumes. A rock band plays cover songs from inside a tent decorated with red and green lights. Staffed tables in the middle of the street serve food and drinks while jugglers on stilts roam the crowd. A giant full moon floats overhead.

Two women giggle up to us holding hands, their faces painted entirely in blue, down to their eyelashes. "Will you take our picture?" one says to me.

"What is this?" I ask her, taking her phone while she and her friend throw themselves into a hug and pose.

"It's the San Encanto Holiday Gala." The camera clicks.

"Is it a benefit?" I ask her. "I don't think the flash went off that time. Let me do it again."

"Now you two get in the picture with us," she says, grabbing our hands and pulling us between them. She extends her arm out to take a portrait of the four of us.

"But you'll never see us again," I protest.

I look at my mother and she shrugs and the four of us squeeze together. I lean my head against hers and smile as the camera goes off. Then the two women let go of us and run into the dancing crowd, holding hands. Everyone is so festive. I feel like a chaperone at the prom – though I didn't go to my own prom, so I'm guessing here.

"I think we can get to a bathroom through the tent," I say. We move inside and are pulled forward by the warm hum of the crowd, whose clamorous energy rises and bounces off the billowing walls. Without thinking, I find I have taken my mother's hand, and we glide and push our way around. She stops and points to a booth on the side of the tent.

"I want to get my face painted," she shouts at me over the music.

"Are you joking?"

This from a woman who used to sleep wearing a hairnet. Who won't hang up on a recording because it's rude. Lately she's been fraying at the edges, though, showing flashes of strange rebellion. She plays Dungeons and Dragons at her neighbor Kenneth's house, eating fried chicken and drinking beer from the bottle with his friends. She joined a pétanque club at the community center and now throws hollow metal balls at a wooden one in the park on Sundays, surrounded by old Italian men. And tonight she slips her hand from mine and yells into the ear of a man at the edge of the party, then sits down in a chair. I catch up with her as he begins painting her forehead red, in broad strokes.

"Will this come off?" I ask him.

"What color do you want?" a young woman with a bumblebee

antenna hairband asks me.

"I'm not doing it."

The man brushes my mother's face and throat and the space above her mouth. Her features relax as the color covers her cheeks, her nose, her lips.

"Oh, what the hell," I tell the woman. I sit in a chair next to my mother. "Any color. Surprise me."

I lean my head upwards and she begins drawing her brush across my face in gentle sweeping motions. She holds my hair off of my forehead and traces her fingers around my ears. "Keep your eyes closed," she says. She moves the soft strands down the sides of my nose, my jaw, my neck. Her fingers press in and massage my temples.

My mind drifts to Henry. I wonder if he is working in the garden now, tending to his winter melons, leaning in to smell each one, testing for its ripeness. He likes to garden at night, when it's cool and dark. I see him out there, his flashlight positioned like a lantern, illuminating soft and mossy leaves while his fingers press into the earth. Sometimes I watch him from the kitchen window.

"Open your eyes," the face painter tells me. Her voice startles me. My mother is standing over me, peering down and grinning. Her face is completely red.

The woman holds up a hand mirror and I am astonished by what I see. I blink a few times. My face is painted golden. I turn and examine myself from different angles. My cheeks catch the sparkling lights; my lashes brush the air as they move.

"You're the Tin Man!" says my mother. She grins, her white teeth a bright crack in her tomato head.

"The Tin Man isn't gold," I say. I put the mirror down. "I think there's a bathroom over there." I nod toward the entrance to Nordstrom and press myself up from the seat.

We walk into the store. It's brightly lit, with holiday bunting and bulbous ornaments hanging from the ceiling and gifts in shiny wrapping tucked into every display. People stare at us as we walk through the room, but I don't care; the color and noise and lights and paint have made me feel as if I'm in a dream.

The bathroom is luxurious. It's old and ornate. There's a stall on either side of the room with frosted glass doors, and the sinks and countertops are marble. My mother takes a Benzedrex decongestant inhaler and sticks it up her nostril, a habit she has done for as long as I can remember.

"I thought you were going to wean yourself off those," I say.

"I asked my doctor. He says there's nothing wrong with it."

"I read an article that says that there is. It makes your nasal membranes swell. It's addictive."

"I'll die with swollen nasal membranes, then," my mother says. She sticks the inhaler up her other nostril and sucks in.

I look at her in the mirror. Her face is bright red; her eyelids droop with age. She bares her teeth involuntarily as she tilts her head back and sniffs.

"I think you should come live with me," I say. I have been waiting for the right time to say this. I don't know that I'm going to now until I hear the words coming from my mouth.

"Why would I do that?" she asks.

"I think it would be safer," I say. "You're getting frail and I'm worried about you falling and no one finding you."

"I'm not frail," she says. "I'm in better shape than you are. I've lived in that house for thirty-seven years." She puts the inhaler into her purse. "Besides," she says, "aren't you going to move in with Henry?"

The question startles me. I run cold water over my hands, which look fleshy and naked in contrast to my painted face, then look around for a towel.

"We've never talked about it," I lie.

I don't tell her that Henry does want to move in together. He wants to marry me. I don't tell her that I still sleep with my old friend Ezra every time he comes through town, even though now he's cheating on his second wife with me. I don't tell Henry about that either.

"If I fall and no one finds me," my mother says, "please give my glass animal collection to the Salvation Army."

"I'm not joking, Mom. Why won't you let me help you?"

She turns to me in the bad fluorescent light, and says, "Why do you insist on helping me?"

She goes into the bathroom stall and closes the door behind her. My eyes sting against the gold powder. The room feels airless, ancient, like a marble tomb. I go into the other stall and we both pee and flush the toilet. I come out and wait for her by the sinks.

"*Come on,*" she mutters.

"What's the matter?" I say.

"The toilet won't stop running."

"It'll stop," I say. "It has to stop some time."

She rattles the handle. "Let me in," I say.

She unlocks the stall door and we huddle over the toilet. Water circles in the bowl. We peer into it, her red face next to my gold one.

"Forget it," she says. "It's not our problem."

"We can't leave it like this," I say. "It'll flood."

"It won't flood. Why would it flood? I think it's stopping now," she says.

The water swirls.

"It's not stopping." I jiggle the handle and it comes off in my hand.

"What did you do?" she says.

"Nothing! I barely touched it!" I try to screw it back on but the bolt has fractured. I put my hands on either side of the toilet tank and push it. It wobbles on the floor.

"What are you doing?" my mother asks, her voice rising.

"Something needs to settle in the tank. Something isn't sealing properly."

"You're going to break the whole thing now."

"No, I'm not," I say. "I'm fixing it. You're the one who broke it." I rattle it again and water swells up and spills over the edges of the bowl. It flows onto the black and white tiles, washing over our shoes.

"Good God," my mother says.

"Do something." I say. "Do something!"

"Me?" she says. "What am I supposed to do?"

I turn and face her. She is so small, so old, in this alabaster room. Her brown shoes are planted on the tiles, flat and stalwart, water splashing onto the scuffed leather. Her wool coat hangs from her shoulders as if of its own volition, square like a general, and full of air. I swear I would forgive her if I could remember what it was she has done.

I put the broken handle down on the counter. "Just forget it," I say. "Let's go."

She looks at me as if I might be testing her. Then a sly smile curls her lips.

"After you, Abby," she says.

We leave and move through the sales floor, passing a salesgirl stocking perfume.

"There's a problem with the toilet in the ladies room," my mother says, her eyes alive.

"I'll let someone know," says the girl, not looking up from her task.

We exit to the plaza. The air is cool and the music from the gala washes over us. The full moon glows above us in the sky. I take her hand again and we press into the crowd of dancing revelers. We are two peas in a pod, she and I, two birds of a feather. We are two Christmas globes, red and golden, rising clear into the night.

The Small Earth Guide to Istanbul

Getting There

There is more than one way to get to Turkey, but the path of least resistance is Ataturk Airport in Istanbul, and why fight the tide? Let the sweeping mountain ranges usher you across the vast expanse where there is no time and no space, where there's only white below until white turns to blue and then to desert. Go with it. Leave the dishes in the sink. Leave the fern to turn to paper. Leave your ex-girlfriend's car at the airport. By the time she finds it you'll be nine thousand miles away.

Ataturk Airport: where the teeming voyagers spill out of metal peapods and into the honking cacophony that is Istanbul. Hark the minarets! The glittering Bosphorus! You will not be alone in Turkey; you will never be alone. Helpful guides wash up to the arriving traveler in waves as gentle as an exhalation. A pattering of hands. *Can I take your bag? Taxi, need a taxi? Come outside, mister, follow me outside.* A boy with large brown eyes might approach you – you, bleary-eyed from fourteen mini-bottles of Turkish Airlines whiskey, over ice. Don't judge me, intrepid traveler. A twelve-hour flight divided by fourteen is a mere wetting of the tongue, something to lubricate the dry cabin air.

"Hey mister," the brown-eyed boy might say. "Come this way. My uncle drives a taxi – cheap, not like the taxi line out front. They'll steal from you in the taxi line, but you look tired. Let me take your bag." He checks the luggage tag, looks at you and says, "Robert Zinger." A tiny thing, a boy of nine, ten, it's hard to tell in his oversized khaki pants and tunic. Revel with your bourbon eyes as he hefts your bag with spindly arms and carries it outside, leaning his little boy frame toward the ground. Teeter behind him and out into the cool, forgiving evening air. Let the fertile scent from the Bosphorus drift toward you, envelop your creaking bones, welcome you to a new world, where there are no dying ferns, no Bluetooth harnessed to your ear, no beleaguered editors with succulent thighs who say yes, yes, yes and then delete you like so much deadwood. Follow the boy, follow your bag to an ill-shaven man in a brown sportshirt that strains over his belly as he feeds your suitcase into the dank trunk of a Saab, circa 1995.

Do not let this irony escape you, for that was the year you began as a travel writer: a toss of shiny hair danced across your forehead; you had whimsy in your step and a jaunt in your gait; a certain dimming of your brown eyes made women weak, made them doff their sweaty backpacks and crawl into your sleeping bag at youth hostels in Jaipur, Montenegro, Belgium. Let the record show: a climbing guide to Patagonia; pocket vineyards in Languedoc; aquamarine caverns found only in Croatia – you led intrepid travelers to them all. And Belinda, valiant editor back home, well, she cleaned up the prose. She parsed out the piddling advances. She even wheedled Joe Prentiss, bulbous ass and self-proclaimed magnate of a slowly imploding empire, into signing off on overdrafts when the cash ran low before the Aeroflot made it home. Beguiling Belinda.

But never mind her: any man can be a sucker. Fear not. The

tender folds of Istanbul will still embrace you. And so it is that you find yourself on a soft cushioned seat, with a beaded curtain swaying between you and the fat man in the Saab. Out the window to your right, the azure, snaking Bosphorus. On your left, to your bewilderment, the boy still sits by your side. His mouth is moving. Words come out. "Rug. Rug. Rug. Rug. Rug," he is saying. Do you want to buy a rug, he wants to know. His family has been making rugs for three generations, the finest rugs in Turkey. Bill Clinton bought a rug from him when he was here. You do not want to buy a rug, you tell the boy. You block out his chattering squall and let the words float up toward the roof, which you notice is carpeted itself, a black and white weave, a maze-like pattern, which swirls and eddies as the car spins around yet another cloverleaf. The seat cushion feels like an angel's bosom underneath your cheek, the dampness of your drool like nectar.

Sleep now, intrepid traveler. You have arrived in Istanbul.

Places to Stay

Hotels, hostels, and tucked away pensiones offer travelers a variety of soft landings in this bejeweled city. Skip the luxury high-rises and visit historic Old Istanbul: might I recommend the Royal Sacred Harem Hotel, just across the Galata Bridge with a stunning view of the Aya Sofya. Let Enes, for that is the boy's name, take you by the hand and lead you inside, down an entryway lined with a mosaic of ornately painted tiles, circles within circles of yellow and crimson stars, radiating out and drawing a weary man in.

A bony man in a suit coat and thin tie sits behind the front desk eating corn on the cob from a plate lined with grilled lemon slices. His tie is crusted with green powder, perhaps pistachio dust, an echo from some distantly eaten baklava. A girl of four or five sits beside him, curled on a chair and swaddling a puppy who sleeps heavily in her arms as she eyes you with suspicion. Enes ignores the girl and talks to the man at the counter in Turkish, now a little businessman. He gesticulates as the two negotiate your rate and his commission.

Go approach the girl. Reach your hand out to the puppy. "Can I pet?" ask her. Humans can be so cold, so fickle, but dogs know only loyalty. Scratch the puppy's sleepy head. He blinks his eyes at you, yawns and twitches his lip as he rouses from a dream. "Name?" you ask. The girl stares back at you. "Doggie name?" you say again. Enes and the man behind the counter stop talking. "Babar," Enes says. "Like the lion." Turn to him and smile. "Like the elephant," you correct him. "Like the lion," Enes answers.

Take the puppy from the girl and cradle him in your arms. Breathe in his musky scent. Wag your face in his soft neck, drag your nose behind his downy ear. Feel the girl's eyes upon you. Why do people always think the worst of others? *Ye of little faith.* Pat the dog reassuringly. The girl sits back in her chair, folds her arms, unconvinced.

Ask the counter man the cost for one bed, one night. "US ninety-five dollars," he says. You must negotiate this price. Every offer in Turkey is a mere opening gesture, an invitation to find a common ground. Answer, "Forty dollars." "Ninety-five," says the man. He scrapes at the green powder on his tie with a fingernail, picks up his corn cob and begins to scan a newspaper. Enes spews a torrent of abuse on him and the man does not look up at first, but tightens his brow and slowly pinches his lips. "Eighty US dollars," says the man. Agree to this.

Release the puppy from your grasp and write your name,

looking up only when you hear the young girl scream. See the puppy wriggle on the painted tiles, splayed, dazed and crying from his three-foot freefall to the floor. The girl rushes to the dog and picks him up, sobs in Turkish at the man behind the counter, who looks at you as if you are covered in shit. Don't dogs always land on their feet? You think you have heard this before, though your thoughts may not be flowing clearly. Enes scowls; eyes the dog, the girl, the man, and you, rocking on his feet.

Sign the guest book. Take the key. Follow Enes, who lugs your bag up to your room. Lie down and have a rest, intrepid traveler. There is still much to see.

Shopping

In the morning Enes hovers at your bedside, his soft and pliant hands pressing at your cheeks, your aching head. "Wake up, Mister, wake up," he says. "Let's go buy a carpet."

Carpet-making has a long tradition in Turkey, with hand-weaving techniques traced back to the twelfth century. Listen to the old woman at the showroom as she tells you this. Showroom really overstates it; it clearly is just a house, with a tidy area in the front that's used to pitch the tourists who wind up here, and a giant loom in back, which you see when she opens the door and waves her hand toward it.

A pretty woman sits on a low bench at the loom and she turns toward the door. She indeed weaves a rug. Lush strands hang above her in colorful bunches. Lower your eyes and cant your head just so. Smile at her in greeting, suggesting all that there can be between a pretty girl and a visitor who comes from far away. Hang lightly in the doorway as she stares back at you with blankness. Pulse limply in your own obsolescence.

The girl returns to her work and Yagmur – for that is the old woman's name – shuts the door and beckons you to sit down on the carpeted floor, as she puts milky spiced tea into your cold, cracked hands. "Wool rug," says Yagmur. "Yuzde yuz yun." She presses your palm along the pile. "Oil, natural. Small knot. Fine and shiny."

Say, "It feels like cotton blend."

"It's wool," says Enes, indignant. He sits cross-legged behind you sipping tea. He plucks a few stray fibers from the fringe and snaps his fingers at the woman, who pulls out a lighter that says "Blue Star Ferries" from the folds of her heavy skirt. Enes takes the lighter and flicks it to a flame and sets the strands in his fingers on fire. "Smell!" he says. "Wool!" Smell the burning fibers. "Wool," you admit, though you have no idea. Yagmur pulls a handkerchief from another hidden fold in her skirt and spits into it. She rubs the wet cloth on the carpet and holds it to your face. "The colors don't run. Good dye." She smiles at you then, her teeth yellow but straight and her face round. "High quality," she says. "You buy."

"I don't need a rug," you confess. "I have a studio apartment. I am a freelance writer."

"Buy it for your wife," says Yagmur.

"I have no wife," you tell her. "I have no girlfriend. I had a girlfriend, but she slept with Joe Prentiss and she's not my girlfriend anymore."

"Buy it for your girlfriend," Yagmur tells you.

Feel the softness of the fibers, let the intricate patterns of third eyes and Turkish Junipers start to sway. Let an image flutter through your mind of Belinda naked on this carpet. She moans, rolls around on its mosaic, cries out your name in dark, throaty sobs. But no, it's not you she moans for. It's Joe Prentiss's bunioned

feet that stand before her, his fungused toenails digging into the
carpet's vibrant pile.

Tell Enes it's time to go.

"No rug," you say. "No rug."

Entertainment

Enes can sense your soured mood and he leads you out to
the Saab and his waiting uncle. "No girlfriend," says the boy, "no
problem. We'll take a day trip. You'll see." He orders his uncle to
a destination in a rapid-fire exchange. Unroll your window and
close your eyes; sleep, perhaps for hours.

At last, the Saab drops you and Enes at an outdoor arena of
some kind. A festival is underway. Crowds of people, mostly men,
jostle and laugh at the edges while an old man dances to a young
man's caterwauling horn and the bang-bang-banging of a hand-
held drum. Brown nuts roast in black kettles and give off a woodsy
aroma. The old man raises his arms, a hand-rolled cigarette between
his fingers, as he turns and turns, bows and dances and the onlookers cheer. The long metal horn's whine pierces your ears and the
drumbeat thrums. Enes negotiates a deal with the man at the gate,
then pulls you past the revelers and down the dusty aisle of the
arena, where men in green jackets mill about in the center and the
crowd bucks and cheers loudly in their seats.

Finally two elaborately decorated camels are led out into the
arena, draped in magnificent fuchsias, purples, golds. A thousand
tiny mirrors jangle from the fabrics and a thousand tiny bells hang
from those. The beasts huff and flare their nostrils and raise their
hairy lips to expose their giant teeth. The crowd goes wild. Enes
pumps his arms in the air and shouts. He turns to you and bares his

own teeth – baby teeth, you think – with unrestrained glee. "They wrestle!" he says. He hoots and stamps his feet. To be such a boy: the world sits before him like a diamond mine, and in his hands he holds a silver axe.

"What does the other camel do?" you ask Enes. The men lead a smaller camel in front of the decorated two, parade her between them and then draw her back behind the barrier.

"She makes them horny," says the boy. "They fight better now."

A bell rings out and the camels crash into one another, dumb and panting, their heads bowed and necks colliding. They move in circles, one pushing forward, the other stepping back, around and around and around. Spittle flies from their mouths and nostrils and dirt blossoms at their hooves. The drumbeat gets louder and the crowd roars, shouting, fists raised. Raise your fist. Begin to yell along with the crowd. The long metal horns whine and screech as the drumbeat quickens. Choose the camel draped in yellow as your favorite and scream until your voice is gone, stamp your feet, let the waves of exaltation lift your spirits. Grab Enes by the armpits and raise him high above your head as he laughs and yells and waves his hands in the air.

The camel draped in purple finally stumbles, his knees buckling beneath him, and he falls. A groan escapes his chest and it's quickly drowned out by the roaring crowd. Laugh until the tears run down your cheeks. He is on the ground now, pinned by the victor, while the men in green coats move in with their ropes and hooks. Shout and dance and holler until you see it. The vanquished camel's face, pressed into the dirt, huge and woolly. His dark eyelashes blink against the dust; his black beaded eye, deep and moist, peers directly at you. It is quiet then, just you and the camel, his soft brown nostrils flaring and his heart beating gently in his massive chest. Feel the fire drain from your body, the elation fall from your limbs, even as you hold Enes above you in the sky.

Istanbul at Night

Istanbul at sunset glitters with the dusky glint of goldstone; the babbling of calls and conversations rises through the open windows back at your hotel. Bow your head over a plate of saffron curry Enes has brought you. Let the steam and piquant spices wet your skin, dampen your eyes, warm your throat. Tomorrow you will leave Istanbul. Tonight: a room, a desk, a spotty internet connection to send back home a manuscript. Let the record show that you have met your obligation: three thousand words, on time, as always. You have never missed a deadline. You have never made a promise you couldn't keep. Perhaps that meant you made scant promises, but it serves no one to overthink these things. You see Belinda now, her lip trembling as she sits on your rumpled bed, her nostrils quavering with apology. What was it that she said? *Don't go*, it may have been. Or was it *don't be such an asshole*. In the end, does the difference matter?

At the front desk, Enes talks to the bony man with pistachio dust on his tie. The man won't look at him, won't give him his attention, keeps his eyes on the newspaper he holds between them. Enes presses the paper down and their voices spark into an argument. Enes puffs out his chest and the bony man speaks to him sharply. Enes begins to cry. The stir lifts your head from its torpor. "Hey," you say. The man waves his hand and lifts his paper, and Enes stands adrift, not a shrewd operator, but a tear-streaked little boy.

The bubbles pip and fizz in your Carlsberg beer. This is not your business. And yet you call the child over. "What happened?" you ask. "Nothing," says Enes. "He broke a deal." It's his commission, you comprehend. It's the price of you. Enes wipes his nose with his sleeve. Sit there silent as a lamppost as he snivels. Dusk has settled in now and amber light from sconces washes the walls. The boy raises his gaze and meets yours. Don't blow this, intrepid traveler. It is that rarest of gifts: A second chance. *What would a kind person do at a time like this?* Reach; think. And then… yes, there it is. Slowly push the plate of yellow curry toward him. Enes takes your fork and tastes the saffron rice, chewing slowly in his dewy cheeks. The boy lifts his hand and rests it quietly on top of yours, pats it gently three times. Now, was that so hard? *There, there.* Why do you feel like crying? Blood pulses through your ropy veins beneath his tiny fingers.

Getting Away

Ah, there's no getting away, now is there, intrepid traveler. Did you really think there was? Wherever you go, there you are. Now the wings of Turkish Airlines spread wide and lift you home. The minarets reach up and wave their plaintive goodbyes. The azure Bosphorus coyly curves around and sends you off with a sly twinkling of light. Let Istanbul release you and grow faint, become a memory before the first whiskey coats your throat. You can't curse a man to smallness, to parochialism. Let him wake each day feeling weightless, his eyes cracking open to the sunlight. The world is wide with possibility. Stay in the fishbowl of your circumstance and you'll miss all of its wonder.

And where is the beauty in that?

ACKNOWLEDGMENTS

This book took a long time to write and a lot of people helped me along the way. Friends first: Tom Barbash, Susan Campbell, Marianna Cherry, Grant Faulkner, Jen Frances, Alastair Gee, Rachel Howard, Vanessa Hua, Carolyn Hubbard, Elizabeth Gonzalez James, Eliza Kent, Joe Loya, Kathryn Ma, JD Moyer, Lynn Mundell, Caroline Paul, Miriam Pirone, Jason Roberts, Tania Schwartz, Aish Shukla, Kia Simon, Julia Scheeres, Meghan Ward. Residencies where several of these stories were written: Cyndy Hayward and the Paella crew at Willapa Bay AIR; Playa Summer Lake; Writing Between the Vines. Dear friend and writing partner Ericka Lutz, whose thoughtful insights are indelible on these pages. Melanie Gideon, for decades of encouragement, friendship, walks, and talks. Jenny Pritchett for her astute read. The journals that first published these stories, especially Ronald Spatz at *Alaska Quarterly Review*, Claire Boyle and Amanda Uhle at *McSweeney's*, and Noah Sanders at *The Racket*. Dominique Lambert-Blum for steadfast support. "The Letter Ladies/Women Who Get Things Done." The Creative Writing department at SFSU, especially Maxine Chernoff and Chanan Tigay. Jonathan Lethem, for seeing potential in my early work and setting the direction of my writing life more than he may know. My agent Henry Dunow, for believing in a quirky

ing with it. Diane Goettel at Black Lawrence Press for giving the book a warm home. Zoe Norvell for designing my wonderful cover. Sorely missed but never far away: Maia Hansen, Victor Martinez, Kirk Stoller. My family, thank you for everything: Nell Bernstein, Timothy Buckwalter, Nicholas Buckwalter, Ruby Buckwalter. All the wonderful Levys, Sokoloffs, Steinbergs and Freymanns. My mom, Harriet, and my dad, Phil. And Jeffrey Freymann, for teaching me patience, absurd swear words, love, and peace. Thank you.

Bay Area native ELIZABETH STIX's stories have appeared in *McSweeney's*, *Tin House*, *Boulevard*, and *The Los Angeles Times* Sunday magazine and have been performed live on public radio's Selected Shorts. She has contributed to numerous anthologies, including *Best Microfiction 2019*, *Drivel*, and *642 Things About You (That I Love)*. In the early 2000s, she founded the vanguard lit zine *The Big Ugly Review*. She has a BA from Brown University and an MA and MFA from San Francisco State University. When she's not writing, she can be found staying up way too late doing the NYT Spelling Bee.

20

R. 1. 2